'You know thi... thing?' Matt sa...

Steffi nodded. 'Hmm...

They settled back, side-by-side, leaning into each other.

His voice dropped lower, found a husky note. 'Is it the done thing for the boy to tell the girl he thinks she's beautiful?'

'I think I read in the manual that's okay.'

He traced a finger along the contour of her cheekbone, sliding it down to her jaw, stroking the soft skin just below her ear. 'What does it say the girl does when the boy tells her that he wants, very much, to kiss her?'

She shook her head. 'I don't think,' she said, her voice barely a whisper, 'there was anything about that.' The suspense was delicious.

'Shall we update the edition?'

'Yes. Please...'

Emily Forbes is actually two sisters who share a passion for reading and a love of writing. Currently living three minutes apart in South Australia, with their husbands and young families, they saw writing for Medical Romance™ as the ideal opportunity to switch careers. They come from a medical family, and between them have degrees in physiotherapy, psychology, law and business. With this background they were drawn to the Medical Romance series, first as readers and now also as writers. Their shared interests include travel, cooking, photography and languages.

Recent titles by the same author:

THE CONSULTANT'S TEMPTATION
CITY DOCTOR, OUTBACK NURSE

OUTBACK DOCTOR IN DANGER

BY
EMILY FORBES

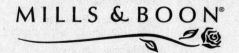
MILLS & BOON®

To Dad—Thank you for encouraging us
to believe that we can do anything.

With thanks to the guys at Sockburn Fire Station,
Christchurch, New Zealand, for their help in researching this story.
Especially, Dave, Paul, Ray and Mark on Brown Watch.

*First published in Great Britain 2005
Harlequin Mills & Boon Limited,
Eton House, 18-24 Paradise Road, Richmond, Surrey TW9 1SR*

© Emily Forbes 2005

ISBN 0 263 84284 3

*Set in Times Roman 10½ on 12 pt.
03-0105-50912*

*Printed and bound in Spain
by Litografía Rosés, S.A., Barcelona*

CHAPTER ONE

'WHAT the hell was that?'

Dr Matt Zeller and Air Ambulance Service pilot Ryan Fitzpatrick felt the tarmac shake under their feet as a huge explosion erupted. As one, they turned to look in the direction of the noise, squinting against the afternoon sun across the narrow stretch of water separating the airport from the town of Port Cadney. For a moment they froze in disbelief at the sight that met their eyes—a huge fireball erupting into the sky, shooting flames and thick, billowing smoke hundreds of feet into the air.

An eerie silence followed the deafening sound of the initial explosion. It must have lasted just for a second or so but it seemed the whole of Port Cadney might have been blown apart, leaving only the fire. The men stood transfixed, mesmerised by the sight of the massive flames. The seagulls, silent for the last few seconds, began to screech and the everyday sound galvanised Matt into action.

Even before Matt had covered the short distance to the base office, next to the small airport terminal, he heard the sirens of the emergency vehicles heading for the accident site. Hopefully there wouldn't be too many casualties but there was no way of guessing. He had no idea what had just happened.

He flung open the door of the office, heading straight for Sheila's desk, the base manager looking up from her conversation on the two-way radio.

'Hang on, Abbey, Matt's just got back. Over.' She took

5

a deep breath and blew it out with force. 'The explosion is at the wharf. I haven't got any more details but they're calling for as many medical personnel as we can reach. Davina will wait here for any calls we get. Can you head across to the docks?'

'On my way.'

Matt ran to his car, his long legs making short work of the distance, and dived into the driver's seat, thrusting the key into the ignition. For once his old car started without any complaints. He pressed his foot down hard on the accelerator and his car shot out of the parking bay, sending a shower of dirt and stones behind it. It would take him ten minutes to make his way to the bridge across the gulf and then back down the other side to the wharf area.

He drove with his window down to get some relief from the unseasonably hot day. Crossing the bridge, he had an unobstructed view of thick clouds of black smoke rolling out over the water. The stench was extraordinary, and he was still a good five-minute drive away. What was burning to make the air thick with such a smell? Rubber? Fuel? Paint?

Pulling into the wharf area, he realised the smoke wasn't as thick here as he'd expected. The wind was blowing away from the wharf, taking a lot of the smoke with it. What was more worrying was the number of people down here. Port Cadney was a small town, population fifteen thousand, but many of the families made their living from fishing so it was not surprising so many were here, trying to find out what had happened. But would emergency personnel be able to keep onlookers from making their job more difficult?

Matt saw Tom Johnston through the crowd and drove through the path the police chief cleared for him. Tom leaned down to speak to him through his lowered window, passing Matt a fluorescent orange, all-weather jacket at the same time.

'What happened?' Matt asked.

'An explosion on one of the trawlers. That's about all we know at this point but they'll be glad of another pair of hands. You'll have to park there…' Tom indicated an area beside an old warehouse '…and make your way to the front on foot. Careful how you go—there's a lot of debris.'

Getting out of the car, Matt hauled the jacket on as he headed towards the emergency vehicles, their red and blue lights flashing through the haze. The smoke grew thicker as he neared the accident site but it wasn't enough to impede breathing—just enough to make him wish he didn't have to smell the stench.

He ran. More of a hop, really, trying to avoid the shards of glass and fragments of metal and wood that littered the wharf, those he stepped on cracking and snapping beneath his feet. Hundreds of dead fish also lay amongst the debris, their shiny, slippery bodies more lethal to a running medic than the detritus of the boat. The trawler must have just come in with a big catch, and the fish would have been sent flying with the force of the explosion. The wharf always smelt of fish but already the odour was worse—the smell of burnt fish mixed with the fumes of the fire was foul.

As he reached the group of vehicles forming a make-shift treatment site, he slid to a stop, his attention caught momentarily by the spectacular sight of the burning fishing trawler, still a hundred metres or so away. He'd never seen such a massive fire. Flames with a terrifying life of their own were wrapping around the trawler's enginehouse and stern, consuming the boat in a gigantic bonfire. Even from this distance, Matt could feel the heat, intense on his skin, over and above the heat of the day and hear the roaring of the flames, punctuated now and then by smaller explosions and voices calling out above the noise. Several other boats had already moored for the night and the flames had spread to boats on either side, leaping across the narrow gaps from one boat to another. Firefighters were tackling the blaze from each end, trying to stop the destruction. Trawlers that were, as yet, unaffected were being moved out of harm's way to more distant moorings.

A voice brought his focus back to his current role. 'Glad you're here.' Stuart Davis, one of the consultant general surgeons, was kneeling next to a prostrate figure, inserting a drip into a forearm.

'This guy's bleeding heavily from stomach wounds.' His voice was controlled but there was an urgency about the way he spoke, an economy of words that spoke volumes. 'I'll have to operate ASAP. There's one confirmed casualty…' he nodded towards a nearby stretcher draped with a full-length sheet '…many injured and a few still unaccounted for. A couple of kids are bleeding badly. Connor could use a hand.' He jerked his head towards the paramedic.

'Got it.' Matt headed in Connor's direction just as Stuart called for a second paramedic to load his patient into the ambulance.

Connor was treating an old fisherman and Matt recognised him as the owner of one of the fishing boats. The man was half lying against a bollard, looking very grey. Connor had applied a cervical collar and was checking the patient's blood pressure, and although the man was bleeding from a deep gash above one eye, the paramedic was ignoring that. Matt knew from the patient's colour that there was more going on than a superficial head wound and Connor obviously thought so, too.

'How does it look?' he asked as he squatted down beside them.

'BP 180 over 110, heart rate 180. He was complaining of left-sided chest and shoulder pain.' Connor didn't take his eyes off his patient who was now having difficulty breathing.

'Get him into the ambulance—we need to get a trace on him.'

Together, they transferred the fisherman to the ambulance on a spinal board, ripping open his flannel shirt to attach the ECG electrodes. His skin was cool and clammy.

'Atrial fibrillation,' Matt said as the signal appeared on the screen. 'Does he have a history of heart problems?'

Connor shook his head. 'No. I've checked that.' He fitted an oxygen mask over the man's mouth and nose to assist his breathing and then grabbed an IV cannula from a nearby container. 'Insert the line for me,' Connor said as he stepped aside to retrieve the necessary medications.

Matt slid the cannula into place in the back of the fisherman's hand just as Connor returned, lifting the oxygen mask and slipping half an Anginine tablet under the patient's tongue. Drawing up five milligrams of morphine and some digoxin, he showed Matt the drugs before handing him the syringe so he could inject the drugs through the IV line.

'You'd better get him to hospital now,' Matt said, climbing out of the ambulance. Connor nodded, one eye on the monitor, the other on their patient, clearly waiting to see if his heartbeat regulated.

He slid the door closed, leaving Connor to monitor the patient on the trip to hospital. As the volunteer ambulance officer in front switched on the siren and drove away, Matt turned back towards the carnage, scanning the scene for the next most critical case.

He flicked a glance to the trawler, concern pricking his mind at the sight, the fire still raging and towering above the firefighters. They seemed to be getting control over the fire at each end of the burning row of boats, but if the wind changed direction there was no telling how quickly the flames would spread to the buildings along the wharf.

'Matt? Are you Matt?'

He looked down and saw a petite, fair-haired stranger at his side. She was wearing a bright orange medical jacket, too, but hers swamped her tiny frame. He felt the air rush out of him as he met her eyes.

'Are you Matt?'

He shook his head, trying to loosen his tongue, then realised she thought he was answering her question. 'I mean yes.'

'Lauren sent me to see what you needed. I'm a registered nurse. Steffi.'

His gaze went to Steffi's mouth, and lingered there, almost as if he was lip-reading. 'Lauren?' His brain still hadn't caught up. Her lips looked soft and moist. His gaze stalled for a moment before he lifted his eyes and met hers, big and bright blue. He felt a flash of recognition. But he knew they hadn't met before, he'd remember. They stood there, chaos reigning around them, and he couldn't tear his gaze, or his mind, away from her. She was lovely, lovely to look at, and if he looked away, mightn't she vanish as quickly as she'd come, back into nothingness?

He heard her clear her throat and it snapped him back to reality but left his heart hammering in his chest, and the words that he should be saying, the actions he should be taking, were still eluding him.

'Lauren Harrison.' She answered his last query. 'She told me she works with you.'

Matt found his voice. 'Yes, of course. You're a nurse?'

Steffi nodded and he returned it with a brief nod of his own tousled head. 'OK, follow me.' He walked away, shortening his stride so that this girl with bright blue eyes—Steffi, was that what she'd said her name was?—could keep pace. He was back in work mode and his comfort level regained its equilibrium.

Up ahead he could see Lauren, a flight nurse with the Air Ambulance Service, treating another victim. With her was Dr Jack Montgomery, her fiancé. A paramedic was attending to a second patient but, from what Matt could see, he didn't require any assistance. A third man was sitting alone, holding a blood soaked towel against the side of his head.

Jack looked up as Matt approached, not wasting time with greetings. 'Could you take a look at Simon here?' He indicated the young man holding the sodden towel to his head. 'He's the next most urgent.'

Matt knelt down and pulled on a pair of disposable gloves with ease.

'Hi, I'm Matt, I'm a doctor and this is Steffi.' Mentally he crossed his fingers that he had her name right. She didn't correct him so he filed her name away and continued, 'She's a nurse and we're just going to have a look at your head.'

He removed the towel for just a moment. Blood was flowing from the man's ear, running down his neck and soaking the collar of his shirt.

His earlobe was gone, neatly sliced off by some flying debris—a piece of metal, Matt assumed. The wound wasn't life-threatening or difficult to deal with, but Matt thought it best not to go into too much detail about the injury with the patient. Shock could be more dangerous than anything else in these situations.

'If you like, I'll fashion a bandage to stem the bleeding

and get him organised for a transfer. You can see to someone else then,' he heard Steffi say.

It made perfect sense. His expertise wasn't required for this job—a nurse was more than capable. But he was reluctant to walk away. 'Are you sure?'

She raised an eyebrow at him. 'I realise you don't know me from Adam but I'm perfectly able to do this, and meanwhile we're wasting time.' Her expression made it clear that *he* was the one wasting time.

'Of course.' As she reached for the kit of supplies she had brought with her, Matt stepped back but he lingered to watch as she selected dressings, plasters and compression bandages. He listened to her soft voice reassuring Simon as her small hands worked to stem the bleeding.

She was right, he didn't know her from Adam, but she seemed to know what she was doing. She was also doing a great job of ignoring his presence but she didn't appear to be offended that he was watching her, checking out her claim to have credentials. He couldn't fault her treatment, couldn't fault anything he'd seen about her so far, in fact. So he should really get going now that he'd satisfied himself of her ability.

A call for help sliced through the air. 'Is there anyone spare? There's an injured man down below.' A fireman had called out from one of the blackened boats tied to the wharf. Matt didn't wait for him to call a second time, heading for the fishing boat as fast as he could.

'What have you got?' There was no need for introductions. In a community of this size most of the medical and emergency services personnel knew each other, at least by sight.

'Young bloke down in the cold room, complaining of leg pain, says he can't stand. I didn't want to move him without someone checking him over.'

'How come he's only just been found?'

'He was listed as missing but no one's been able to check this boat because of the fire. Says he's been calling out but obviously he couldn't be heard over the noise of the firefighting equipment.'

It was only then that Matt realised the noise level had dropped, even though he was now right by the trawler. The firemen had finally got the inferno under control and now just one boat was still burning but much less fiercely. Others were still smouldering, including the one Matt was looking at, two berths away from the centre of the blaze.

The big boat was badly damaged, its forward deck buckled and charred, and the thick, putrid smell of the smoke was still heavy all around them. Not to mention the reek of thousands of dead fish strewn all about, the stench cranking up as the hot sun burned down on them. But the fire was under control and further catastrophe had been averted.

He looked warily at the remains of the boat. The fire had spread to the rear of the deck, too, and although the damage didn't look as bad, he wasn't about to go charging in. The first rule of medical training was to ensure you'd assessed the risks to yourself. He'd be no good to anyone if he ignored the rules.

'Safe to go on?'

'Follow me.' The firefighter headed towards the rear gangplank, which was unscathed, whereas the forward one was a charred mess. They crossed onto the boat.

'The stairs take you into the cold room. I'll stay up here. We have to be careful the wind doesn't whip any embers back up.'

'Cheers,' Matt muttered under his breath as he grabbed the handrail. So much for assessing risk. They might always assess but they also went right on ahead no matter what answer they got.

He called out to the retreating fireman, 'Can you send someone else as soon as they're free? I might need a hand.'

The response came floating down to him as he slid down the steps. 'Sure thing.'

He picked his way over the slippery floor, awash with water that would have gushed in from the hoses. The fisherman was sitting on the wet floor, holding his left knee.

'G'day. I'm Matt. Can you tell me your name?'

'Bobby.'

'Do you remember what happened?'

'Not really. I think I must have missed a step and fallen down here. Next thing I knew, I was lying on the deck.'

He obviously didn't recall the explosion. Had the blast sent him flying?

'Did you sit yourself up?'

'Yeah, I was going to get up but my ankle is killing me. There's no way I could stand. I can't move now, it hurts too much.'

'I need to check you over before we move you any further. Does anything other than your ankle hurt?'

'I've got a bit of a bump on my head,' Bobby ran his hand gingerly over his right temple, 'but that's nothing compared to this damn ankle.'

Matt dug a small torch out of the medical kit and shone it into Bobby's eyes one at a time. Bobby had had a brief LOC but there didn't appear to be any major head injury. He'd also managed to sit himself up so he probably hadn't suffered any major spinal damage. Matt needed to look at his ankle but first he had to get Bobby's waterproof overalls, with all-in-one thick rubber boots attached, off. He looked around and spotted a knife handle protruding from a knife belt around Bobby's waist.

'Can I borrow that?' He pointed to the knife. 'I need to cut your boot and overalls away.'

Bobby flicked open the strap holding the knife in place and passed it, handle first, to Matt.

The filleting knife was razor sharp and Matt slit Bobby's overalls at the knee before running the knife carefully through the fabric down towards the boot. The rubber of the boot was much thicker and he had to use a sawing action with the knife to cut through it. As he was working, a pair of feet and denim-clad legs appeared next to him. He stopped cutting and looked up, smiling automatically when he saw Steffi standing there.

She had a silver space blanket in one hand and a pair of heavy-duty shears in the other. 'Try these, they might be easier,' she said, handing them to Matt. 'What would you like me to do?'

'Bobby had a brief LOC. He's complaining of a bump on the head. Can you check him out? The bump might have knocked him out or he might have just blacked out with the pain. He seems fairly alert now.'

Matt took the shears Steffi held out for him. Their hands touched and a bolt of awareness shot up his arm. Not that unexpected given his earlier reaction to her but, still, this was hardly the time or the place.

Steffi jumped as his touch seared her skin. Her hands were shaking—circumstances, not her reaction to this man, she told herself. She wrapped the insulated blanket around Bobby's shoulders and started to palpate his skull. Her life was a big enough mess already. She didn't need to compromise her work because she had the hots for some stranger in an orange jacket.

She tried to block it out, tried to block him out, as she introduced herself to Bobby. But Matt was right in front of her and she didn't need to watch what she was doing. Her fingers would find any lumps or bumps on Bobby's head, so she could watch Matt without too much difficulty. It wasn't checking him out, more like plain old professional curiosity. Tit for tat. He'd certainly spent more than a moment watching her when she'd treated Simon.

He wielded the shears with confidence, pulling the rubber of the boot apart and easing it away from Bobby's leg and foot, his touch gentle and sure. He might not have a traditional doctor's haircut, his hair falling to his shoulders in soft waves, but he certainly had doctor's hands. Lovely hands. Caressing, strong hands, hands that would sense the tiniest detail. She caught herself just before she licked her lips. That might not be so professional.

'Did you find anything?'

Steffi jumped as his voice brought her attention back to the job at hand. 'No, nothing. Do you want me to do his obs?' Bobby had gone quiet and she knew that, like most of the victims today, shock was bound to set in.

'Thanks.' Matt turned back to Bobby, continuing his examination of an ankle that was bruising and swelling even as they watched.

'I think he may have a crush fracture of the calcaneus,' he said, as Steffi slipped a thermometer under Bobby's tongue.

'Pulse 140, temperature normal,' she reported.

Matt was now examining Bobby's pelvis. She knew a fall heavy enough to shatter a heel could also damage the spine, pelvis and hips. Bobby was managing to sit, though, so it looked as if he was relatively lucky, although he might disagree, Steffi thought as she reached for the blood-pressure cuff. As she was about to pick up the cuff, the medical kit slid out from under her hand, as if pushed by an invisible force. She watched it slide along the floor to the opposite bulkhead smacking into it with a resounding thud. She was swaying to keep her balance but time seemed to be slowing down. She couldn't get a handle on what was happening here.

Matt's reaction was faster. He braced himself against a freezer with one foot and threw his weight across Bobby's upper leg, preventing him from sliding, too.

'Get off the boat, Steffi. *Now.*'

CHAPTER TWO

'WHAT'S going on?'

'Just get off the boat.'

Matt's tone brooked no argument but Steffi still tried to stretch towards the medical kit before heading for the steps.

'Leave it.'

It was an order and for a moment she bristled, but then it sank in that he thought the situation was serious. When she started to clamber up the steps the boat tilted further and she missed her footing, falling back down. She realised Matt had been right. The situation *was* serious.

He called out to her, 'Are you OK?'

'I'm fine.' She grabbed the handrail and started to haul herself back up the stairs, which were now tilted at a thirty-degree angle to the starboard side.

'The boat's taking in water.' There was an urgent note in his voice and she looked back down to see dark water seeping across the floor, more than just the water that had collected here from the fire hoses.

'I'll call for help,' she said as she hurried up the stairs as best she could, but as she reached the top and swung herself onto the deck, she knew Matt was right behind her. Turning, her jaw dropped open as she saw him climbing the last few steps with their large-framed patient slung over his shoulder in a fireman's lift. He was showing no sign of strain, despite having to counter the weights of both of them against the list of the boat, but Bobby was looking paler than ever. He'd be in a great deal of pain, Steffi knew, but Matt had clearly not wanted to wait for a stretcher.

Matt grunted at her, which she took to mean she should get moving, but she stood aside to let him take Bobby off first then picked her way over the deck, almost dropping to a crawl when the trawler lurched further on its side. She felt strong hands grab her under her armpits and lift her onto the wharf. Relieved, she looked up to see one of the firefighters standing before her.

'Thank you,' she said, covering her moment of disappointment that it hadn't been Matt.

Then she stood to the side, watching Matt and Connor, who had returned from the hospital. By the time they had Bobby lying on a stretcher, he'd fainted again.

'He's fractured his right calcaneus, he's in shock but otherwise OK.'

Matt's voice rang out clear and controlled as he issued instructions and handed the patient over to the ambulance officers. Among the competing sounds, his voice was the only one that penetrated her awareness.

He was still talking to Connor. 'Check his BP and give him some pain relief. He'll need X-rays of his spine, pelvis and lower limbs. He doesn't appear to have sustained a head injury but someone will need to check that again.'

'No worries.' Connor whisked Bobby into the ambulance just as Jack and Lauren arrived, the look on Lauren's face showing her relief that Steffi was safely off the trawler.

Jack clapped Matt on the back. 'That's it, all done. Your patient was the last missing person and your timing was impeccable.'

Matt looked at him in query.

Lauren answered, 'You ended the day on a fittingly dramatic note. Sinking ship and all that.' They turned to look at the ailing trawler, blackened and charred and now listing sadly to starboard, incongruous against a sky streaked with gold now that the sun was low on the horizon, daylight fading fast.

Matt threw his gloves into the bag that Jack was holding out for him. 'We'll be needed in Theatre?'

'Looks like it.'

'What was the final toll?'

'Two casualties at the last count, Brian Price and Johnno Mundy. It was his boat that went up,' Jack replied. 'There were a number of relatively minor wounds from flying metal, one heart attack, the stomach wound, a fractured ankle, a dislocated shoulder and some fractured ribs.'

'Any idea what actually happened?'

'Looks like a refuelling accident but the police and fire brigade will have to piece things together before we'll know for sure.'

'It could have been a whole lot worse. They were lucky today,' Lauren said. Turning to Matt and motioning at Steffi, she said, 'I see you've met my big sister.'

'Your sister?' Matt looked from one to the other and Steffi knew the differences between them were jumping out at him. Lauren was tall, dark-haired and long-limbed with a generous bust while Steffi was almost her exact opposite, small and fair-haired. But they had the same olive skin and their eyes were almost identical. His eyes connected with Steffi's and she saw the same spark of recognition he'd shown when they'd first met. He had recognised her eyes, the same deep, striking blue as Lauren's.

He extended his right hand towards her. 'I don't believe we've been properly introduced. I'm Matt Zeller.'

She couldn't ignore his outstretched hand but she really didn't want her sharp-eyed sister to see her go all gooey. She placed her hand in his. Yup, there it was, that tingly sensation shooting up her arm and then down through the rest of her. A shower of little drops of heat.

'Steffi Harrison,' she said, and pulled her hand away. Checking the guy out was one thing, but heart-stopping tremors were quite another. She didn't have room in her life for sexual attraction. And she had enough evidence of how out of control her mind and body already were at the moment. She didn't need more reactions she couldn't control.

If Matt noticed her abrupt withdrawal, his expression didn't change. 'Good work today,' was all he said.

He was assessing her, she thought. But professionally or personally, she didn't know.

'Thank you.'

'Good job all round,' said Jack, before turning his attention to Matt. 'I don't think our work is done yet. Can you give me a ride to the hospital in that old bomb of yours?'

Matt laughed and his face lit up, softening the angular lines of his features, and Steffi's stomach took another tumble. Hot, hot, hot seemed to be the only words her mind could formulate.

'Sure. Let's go.'

'I'll see you later,' Jack said to Lauren, kissing his fiancée firmly on the lips.

The kiss was going on a little too long, Steffi thought. Especially when all she could think about was how lovely it would be to be kissed like that...by Matt. She felt him watching her and smiled, raising her eyes heavenwards to cover her embarrassment at the two of them standing around, waiting for her sister and Jack to finish.

Jack pulled away and said, 'We should be making tracks.'

Goodbyes said, Matt and Jack headed back along the wharf, leaving Steffi and Lauren. They watched the two men, stripping off their waterproof jackets as they went, deep in conversation.

'I love to watch him walk away,' Lauren said.

Steffi looked at Lauren to explain.

'He's got such a great butt,' she clarified.

Steffi looked again, but not at Jack. She couldn't help it. She'd better try distraction. 'Come on. I need a shower and a change of clothes.'

'Are you coming back to my place?'

'I really need to get back to Mum and Dad's. Jess will be wondering what's happened to us.'

Steffi dropped Lauren at her unit in town before heading out to their parents' station, sixty kilometres north of Port Cadney. She pulled up to the rambling homestead and shook her head. To think she'd come back to the country for some peace and quiet.

Inside she found her mother and her daughter surrounded by old family photo albums, laughing hysterically at the pictures.

'I thought you were supposed to be packing,' Steffi said to her mum as she bent to kiss Jess.

'You know what it's like. We got a bit sidetracked when we started to clean out the storeroom. How did it go?'

'Better than it could have. There've been two casualties

but it could've been much worse, given the extent of the blast.'

'Why don't you go and get cleaned up while Jess and I tidy these things away?'

Steffi didn't need to be asked twice. It was bliss to stand under a hot shower, thinking about the day. A day that should have been spent helping Lauren with her wedding plans, not assisting with a major rescue operation.

But it was probably a good thing she'd been so busy. She hadn't felt even the slightest hint of the panic attacks that had plagued her recently. She hadn't had time to think about anything. Was that why? Whatever, at least she hadn't fallen apart in front of Matt. If anything, she'd taken control, at least when they'd first met.

Warmth welled up inside her at the thought she'd impressed him today. Not that that mattered. He was no one to her, played no role in her life. What role could men ever have other than to cause trouble? Right now, trouble was the one thing she had in abundance. She didn't need any more. And trouble that strolled in looking like a rumpled sea pirate, all windblown, wavy hair and long, lean limbs, was trouble with a capital T.

'Ready when you are, Matt.'

Matt made a vertical incision through the skin on the anterior aspect of Alex Carter's left shoulder. His dislocated shoulder had been reduced at the wharf but Toby Maguire, the visiting orthopaedic surgeon, had suspected anatomical damage. X-rays, taken from a superior view, confirmed a fragment of cartilage had separated from the glenoid rim, meaning Alex had to be opened up so they could take a look inside.

Stuart, the general surgeon, was in the other theatre,

stitching up the patient who had sustained stomach wounds, and Jack was in a treatment room removing a fragment from another victim's eye.

Matt's incision had penetrated the skin and he now separated the deltoid and pectoralis major muscles to expose the coracoid process, the bony anterior projection of the shoulder blade.

'I'm in.'

Toby came over to have a look. 'OK. If you hold the retractors I'll take a look at the damage.'

Matt picked up the small retractors and held Alex's shoulder muscles out of the way, giving Toby a clear field of vision. Toby cut through the bony coracoid, deflecting it downwards along with its attached muscles.

'What have we got here?' He surveyed the damage, speaking out loud for the benefit of his theatre team. 'Torn anterior capsule plus a detached labrum. Let's get to work.' He reattached the labrum and capsule to the glenoid rim before replacing the coracoid process. 'Can you close him up for me?'

Matt sutured the wound neatly before putting Alex's arm into a sling to hold it against his stomach over the next few weeks.

'It was lucky for him you were torn away from your clinic at Port Lincoln and flown back to help out today,' Matt said. 'The recovery process in this case is slow enough, without being sent to Adelaide for surgery.'

'You could have managed this one.'

'I'm happy to tackle surgical cases in an emergency but I'd rather leave non-urgent cases to the experts.'

Matt left Alex in the care of the anaethetist and stripped off the outer layers of his theatre scrubs, throwing them into the laundry bin and disposing of his gloves. He untied his mask and left it hanging around his neck, scrubbing his hands at the sink before going to check on the status of the other accident victims.

The last few minor injuries were being attended to. They were mostly flesh wounds requiring suturing, so he went in search of Bobby.

He found him resting in a ward with IV pain relief and his leg bandaged and elevated to reduce swelling. The general surgeon was at the nurses' station, writing in Bobby's medication chart. Matt leant on the desk, peering over his shoulder.

'What do you think?' Matt asked.

'Calcaneal fractures are difficult cases, as you know. The best chance he's got of getting anything near a full recovery is to let him get early movement so I don't want him restricted in a plaster. I'll ask Toby to view the X-rays before he heads off, but this is usually the preferred action.' Stuart put the chart down and picked up Bobby's case notes. 'Happy to monitor him? It's difficult when I'm only here once a week.'

'Of course.'

'I've ordered physio. Just active bed exercises for the first three or four days. When you're happy, he can stand to get out of bed and start partial weight bearing, the usual thing.'

Matt took the case notes to countersign, scrawling his name in the space for the admitting doctor as the other doctor excused himself. 'I'd better get back to Theatre and whatever remains of my scheduled list. It'll throw the waiting list into complete chaos if I don't get through some of the procedures today.'

Matt headed to the staffroom, hoping for a quick coffee before any more dramas unfolded. He was still on call for the Air Ambulance Service and Sheila could be looking for him at any moment. Jack was already there, sipping his coffee as if it was the sweetest brew he'd ever tasted. Hard on Matt's heels came Pam Fisher.

Jack glanced at Pam. 'You look frazzled. Anything I can do to help?'

'Not unless you're hiding any of my nurses in here,' she said, looking around the staffroom as if hoping to see some more people pop out of the woodwork, but the room was empty except for the three of them. 'You haven't seen Carol by any chance?'

'Not since she helped me patch up Simon's ear. What's the problem?'

'All these new admissions and too many of them are staying. It's almost school holidays so I'm desperately short of nurses anyway and now I need to do some major reshuffling of the rosters.'

Matt asked the obvious. 'Can we send some patients to Adelaide?'

'I wish we could, but I had empty beds and you know what the locals are like. They want to stay close to home. I can't say I blame them but I need to get more nurses from somewhere. I was hoping Carol would be able to think of some.'

'Lauren's sister, Steffi, is back in town on holidays—she's a RN.'

Matt's interest was roused.

'Would she be able to work if she wanted to?' Jack asked.

'As long as her registration is current, she can.' Pam was looking happier. 'Is she employed anywhere else, though? That might pose a problem.'

'I don't think so but don't quote me on that.'

'How long is she here for?'

Matt was aware he was only a fraction away from holding his breath, waiting for Jack's answer.

'At least until the end of the school holidays, after Lauren and I get married. You should've been able to discharge most of this lot by then.'

'As long as we don't have any other big disasters.'

'Shall I ask her to give you a call?'

'That would be terrific, thanks.'

'No problem.'

'Why do you think she'd be interested in working if she's on holidays?' Matt asked as soon as Pam had left the room. 'Surely that defeats the purpose of a holiday?'

'Steffi grew up here. I'm learning that you country people like to help each other, particularly in times of a crisis,' he said, making reference to his and Matt's differing backgrounds. 'And if she's anything like her sister, she won't be able to resist feeling needed.'

Matt hoped he was right.

Steffi's confidence was growing inch by inch as she checked to see which patients she would be nursing today. A short orientation shift at the hospital the previous day had eased her in a little, and now she was due to do her first full shift.

Alex Carter's name was at the top of her list so she decided to start with him. He was less drowsy today, not requiring the same level of pain relief.

'Good morning, Alex. Would you like a wash?'

'Absolutely. I'd love to get this orange stuff off me, whatever it is.'

'It's Betadine. We use it to wash your skin before any incisions are made, to reduce the chance of infection. You do look a bit of a mess with the grime from the accident *and* the Betadine.'

She set about cleaning him up and making him more comfortable.

'How about a shave?' She helped him to dry himself then pull his tracksuit pants on, still an awkward movement for him with his arm in a sling.

He shook his mind. 'Maybe I'll try a beard.' He settled back against his pillow. 'Do you think I'll be allowed to go home today?'

'If you weren't left-handed you might.' She got Alex to bend forward so she could slip his right arm into his T-shirt before pulling it down to cover his left. 'But as your dominant hand is going to be out of action for at least three weeks, I'd expect that you'll be with us for a little bit longer.'

'I'm not going to have to stay in hospital for the whole three weeks, am I?'

'Not enjoying our company, Alex?'

Steffi jumped as a third person joined their conversation. She turned around to see Matt standing by the door, looking clean and fresh compared to when she'd last seen him at the wharf, but still a little rough around the edges. He smiled at her and his slate-grey eyes lit with warmth.

Her heart started racing. At least she wasn't in the middle of shaving Alex. Her hands were shaking so much he would have been bleeding by now.

They greeted him unison. 'Hi, Dr Zeller.'

'Alex. Steffi.' He inclined his head towards her.

Steffi helped Alex settle back against the pillows again but she was conscious of Matt as he walked to the bedside. 'What are you doing here?'

'My ward round.'

'But I thought you were a flying doctor.'

'I am. But anyone admitted to hospital by me is my responsibility, including anyone I operate on, or assist with, too. I'm here on a daily basis, give or take a day here and there.'

Matt returned his attention to Alex. 'Keen to get home, are you? Let me take a look at your shoulder.'

Steffi waited for further instructions while Matt examined his patient, using the time to study him more closely.

He had a strong jaw and well-defined cheekbones, chiselled features. He was dark, intriguing. His hair was longish but it suited his angular features. Tall and lean, he looked like he could use a decent meal, although his broad shoulders saved him from looking undernourished. He was undeniably attractive, maybe not in a classic sense but he definitely had something that made her want to be near him, listen to his voice, shake his hand again. What a pity they couldn't be introduced again. She touched her right palm, remembering the feel of his hand shaking hers at the wharf, his grip firm, warm, strong.

Perhaps because of where they'd first met, she still thought he'd make a good pirate—the handsome rogue. He even had a scar on his upper lip which was only visible in certain lights. He was what people meant by the strong, silent type. Serious, intense maybe. And it helped that he didn't appear to be aware of his good genes. Arrogance wasn't high on her list of appealing character traits in a male. She shook her head to clear the muddled direction of her thoughts. Since when had she had *any* list of appealing male character traits?

Matt was now palpating Alex's shoulder, checking the temperature and feeling for any excess swelling. Steffi knew the wound itself was slightly reddened but nothing more than expected.

He picked up Alex's chart. 'Can you wriggle your fingers for me please?'

Alex attempted to move fingers that were stiff and swollen.

'Have you been doing the exercises the physio showed you?'

Alex nodded.

'As often as she said?' Matt obviously doubted it, and Steffi agreed. Alex's fingers shouldn't be that swollen, and if he had been exercising them regularly they would have to look for other reasons for the swelling.

Alex shook his head. 'It's pretty sore.'

'When you do your wrist and finger exercises?'

'No,' he admitted. 'When I do the elbow and shoulder ones.'

Matt frowned. 'You're not moving your arm when you do the shoulder exercises, are you?' It was too early for Alex to be moving his shoulder joint without damaging the repair site.

'No, just pushing against my other hand to tighten the muscles.'

Alex was supposed to perform some static shoulder exercises and also take his arm out of the sling a few times a day to straighten his elbow, so Steffi knew that was OK.

'Did the physio tell you to do those after pain relief?'

'Yes.'

'The wrist and finger exercises are comfortable?'

Alex nodded again.

'But you're not doing them every hour.'

'I forget.'

'You need to start remembering. I'm not going to dis-charge you with so much swelling, particularly when you're left handed. I'll check you again in the morning and speak with the physio before we make any decisions. Do your exercises, OK?'

'Yes, sir.'

Matt turned to Steffi. 'I won't ask you to police his exercises, he's a grown man….'

Steffi could hear the request just the same. 'It's OK, I'll give him a few reminders but I think having to stay in here will be reminder enough. Isn't that right, Alex?'

'For sure.'

'Good.' Matt turned back to Steffi. 'Any more of my patients on your list?'

'Let me check.' Steffi pulled her list from her pocket. 'Bobby Simpson, he's yours?'

'He is. Shall we see him next?'

She knew she didn't have to follow Matt on his rounds. She also knew she was more than happy to do so, more than willing to extend the contact, even if it was purely for work's sake. Maybe working together at the wharf had created some sort of bond between them. Hadn't she heard of that happening between disaster victims and their res-cuers? Maybe it was true for coworkers, too. Or maybe it was simply chemistry, possibly all one-sided. Whatever it was, she almost felt as though, if he asked, she'd follow him anywhere. Maybe not follow, but certainly walk by his side. She felt safe with him. Quite why that was when her main image of him was as a pirate, she couldn't say. She quickened her step to match his and wondered what her hair looked like today. And knew then that the panic attacks might have been only an initial sign that something was seriously wrong with her mind. She was juggling too many needs at the moment to start giving her hair any sort of priority.

Bobby was in the next ward but, through the window in the corridor, they could see that he was busy with the physiotherapist, so they stopped outside.

'Jack didn't have much trouble persuading you to work with us, I gather.'

'I think he knew to appeal to my sense of community spirit.' Steffi laughed as she spoke and Matt thought he'd never heard a lovelier sound.

'How long will we have the pleasure of your company?'

'At least until Lauren and Jack's wedding. It'll be a good break for us.'

Us? Matt felt a surge of disappointment rip through him. Or was it jealousy? She had a husband. But hadn't she said her name was Harrison, the same as Lauren's?

'Is your husband from around here, too?'

He got a blank look in response to his fishing for information. 'I don't have a husband.'

He was aware of the tension evaporating from his body. Good. One less obstacle. Perhaps the 'us' wasn't very serious after all.

'I have a daughter.'

Matt felt relief shoot through him. A daughter. Steffi was a mother. That was much better than her being a wife. 'How old is she?'

'Almost nine.'

'Nine!' He knew Steffi was older than Lauren so she was at least twenty-six but... 'You couldn't possibly have a nine-year-old child.'

'I do. I started young.'

He thought he could hear a note of regret creep in to Steffi's voice. What was that all about?

'I have a niece in town, Susie, she's eight and a half, going on fifteen. She spends a lot of time with me when her parents are working. Maybe we should get them together?'

'Maybe.'

'I can hear a "but."'

She shrugged. 'I'm just used to making my own arrangements where Jess is concerned.'

'Wouldn't she like some company her own age?'

She shrugged again and didn't meet his eyes. Not quite the enthusiastic response he'd hoped for.

'Why don't you think about it? Maybe ask Jess?' Matt reached down to his belt and pulled his pager off as it started beeping. He glanced at the number. 'I won't be offended if you don't take me up on the offer. My skin's thicker than that.' He knew the grin he shot at her was full of cheek, challenging her to ask Jess and saying he knew full well what Jess's reaction would be.

Matt waited but Steffi didn't respond. He clipped his pager back onto his pocket. 'Think about it?'

'OK.' She added almost as an afterthought, 'Thank you.'

'Good. I'll catch up with you later.' He tapped his pager. 'I'd better go see what this is about.'

Steffi stood still, waiting for the tingles to stop running down her spine. One grin, one genuine smile to crinkle the lines in his face, and she'd gone to mush. She wasn't sure what she'd just agreed to. Introducing her daughter to Susie, Matt's niece, was that all? There was nothing too threatening about that, it was just to give Jess a friend. There was no reason why she wouldn't be able to keep her distance from Matt. There was no indication that Matt was as attracted to her as she was to him, no suggestion he was being anything other than a friendly local, making a gesture of welcome. So there was nothing to worry about.

And if she decided to stay in Port Cadney, the fact that Jess would already have a friend would make the transition easier for them both. She tugged absently at the skirt of her uniform as thoughts of all the things she *really* had to worry about clouded her mind. It seemed like she had her whole life to sort out. In the scheme of things, whether or not she could, or should, get to know Matt surely shouldn't be giving her so much anxiety. But nowadays it seemed she'd worry about anything that stood still for long enough.

CHAPTER THREE

LAUREN put a cup of tea down on the table in front of Steffi, slopping the hot liquid over the edge of the cup before sitting back with her feet on the table, flicking though a bridal magazine heavily tagged with little yellow stickers.

Steffi grabbed a serviette and mopped up the spill. 'What essential items are on the agenda tonight? Retractable heels on our stilettos so we can move from aisle-walking to disco? Toothpicks monogrammed with intertwined initials of the bride and groom?'

Lauren waved her hand to brush the comments aside. 'You think I'm crazy? I sorted all that out weeks ago. All we have to do tonight is make a final decision on the flowers.' She paused. 'And underwear. And jewellery. And you have to help me with my speech.'

'All!' Steffi muttered under her breath. 'Let's get on with it. I've had a long day already.'

Two hours later, the pile of magazines had been discarded and Steffi was paper-clipping together a number of neatly cut pages recording Lauren's decisions.

'Now we've done the important stuff, tell me how your day was.'

Steffi put the papers on the coffee-table before leaning back on the couch and tucking her legs under her.

'Long. Stressful. Tiring. In that order.' *Hot, total turn-on, kissable. In that order.*

'Why stressful?'

'Just having to find my way around somewhere new

with different protocols, different people.' At least, that was the only part she was ready to share.

'Why are you working anyway? You're meant to be here on holidays.'

Images of Matt vanished. Lauren was touching on serious issues now and maybe it was finally time to confide in someone. 'Actually, what I really needed was to get away from my life in the city, have some time to regroup. A longer break from work would be great but I can't afford to pass up the money and at least this gives me a break from the Prince Edward.' She named the hospital she'd been working at for the past few years.

'I thought you were doing well? You always seem fine.'

'Appearances can be deceptive.'

'Want to talk about it?'

'I've been having panic attacks. I hate my job. I can't afford to live in the city.' She screwed her face up as if she'd saved the worst for last. 'And Jess is being bullied at school.'

Lauren's mouth was hanging open.

'Well?' asked Steffi.

'Well, what? Where do I start? I've obviously been a lousy sister, wrapped up in Jack and the wedding. I had no idea.'

'I didn't want you to know. It's never been all beer and skittles in Adelaide. I wouldn't have survived this long if I'd kept unburdening myself to you all. I've just had to get on with things.'

'If you don't want us to know something, you're the master of disguise?'

'Something like that.'

'Don't get me wrong, I'm relieved you've told me but why didn't you tell me before things got out of control?'

'I thought coming home for a few weeks might just take

the pressure off us, give me a chance to sort things out, and it was perfect timing with your wedding. I imagined all I needed was a bit of a break and everything would right itself.'

'And now?'

'It's not so clear cut. I need to think seriously about whether Adelaide is the right place for Jess and me any more.'

'What's not so clear cut?'

Steffi spread her hands out in an encompassing gesture. 'All of it. For a start, the panic attacks haven't just gone away, like I was hoping.'

'Have you had treatment?'

'No, that's partly why I thought it was time I spoke to you. I need your recommendation for someone to see here.'

Lauren didn't hesitate. 'See Nadine Robbins, she's a psychologist. She's very good, works with me with my teenage mother support groups.'

Steffi nodded, mentally filing the name away. 'And I'm finding it harder and harder to make ends meet in the city. I'm working more overtime to survive financially but, as a result, I've not been around much for Jess. It was months before she told me about the bullying. If I'd had more time for her, she would've told me sooner.'

'What happened with Jess?'

'Picked on by a group of girls all last term, you know the type of thing.'

'Not ready to talk about it?'

'Not tonight, I've got to get to bed. I'm working again tomorrow, and you've still got to drive home.'

'You know you do have to keep talking this through with me? I might be a self-obsessed bride-to-be right now, but even I don't think the colour of wedding serviettes is as important as your well-being.'

'Thanks. How do I rate against the dresses and wedding food?'

'Equal first.'

Steffi swatted Lauren on the arm and Lauren leant across on the couch and gathered her up in a hug.

'Thanks.' Steffi's voice was muffled against Lauren's shoulder.

'Any time.' She leant back again. 'And I mean *any time*.' She pinched Steffi on her upper arm for good measure.

'Ow!' Steffi rubbed her arm and laughed. 'You might be about to get married but you're still an annoying little sister.' She felt like rubbing her eyes, too. She was tired but it felt as though a load had been lifted from her shoulders. Maybe she'd made a mistake in hiding behind her mask of being the perfect single parent, endlessly upbeat, energetic and successful at juggling the impossible. She was feeling a little more like her old self than she had in months. A little.

Matt found himself shortening his stride for Steffi to keep pace. She was tiny but athletic, all neat, toned limbs and beautifully in proportion despite being small. And somehow, despite her height, she'd still managed to be blessed with long legs. It had never occurred to him before that petite women could be long-legged relative to their height, but she was. Her legs, brown and smooth, were bare under her knee-length navy and white uniform. He looked across at her and smiled and was glad she was there.

'I never got to check on Bobby yesterday after the call-out. I'm heading that way now. Do you want to join me?'

'Sure.'

Matt knocked on the door and held it open for Steffi to enter, watching how her gold ponytail sat smooth and sleek before flicking out to one side, an endearing little imperfection.

Bobby held up a hand in greeting.

'How are you coming along?' Matt picked up chart and glanced at the notations.

'Not too bad. My ankle hurts like crazy but I guess that's no surprise.'

'Keeping up your pain relief?'

Bobby grimaced.

Steffi was taking his pulse. 'He's being a hero, aren't you? Trying to do me out of a job by refusing any medication.'

'There's no shame in taking something for your pain. In fact, it will enable you to relax and give your body time to start healing. And with the fracture you gave yourself, most men would be pumping the IV line as hard as they could.'

Bobby looked a little appeased. 'Maybe I should have just a bit.'

Matt wrote him up for some painkillers and Steffi took the chart to record his obs before slipping out of the room to fetch the medications.

'You were lucky, all things considered,' Matt said. 'Your fractured ankle is nasty but things could have been a lot worse. How are you feeling generally?'

'OK, I guess. When will I be walking again? And when can I go back to work?'

'I'll be honest with you. On average it's about three months before you can expect to be walking comfortably. And it may be a lot longer before you can spend prolonged periods of time on your feet, if at all. I realise that's imperative in your job but at this stage I'd say you'll have to wait and see. There are no guarantees. I'm sorry.'

Bobby looked gloomy. 'I don't know how to do anything else but I guess I won't have anything to do anyway until the trawler's sorted out.'

'Any news on that?'

'Johnno's trawler is history but I guess he won't be needing it any more anyway. There's damage to six others, enough to stop them going out to sea, which is affecting everyone's income. Such a stupid thing to have happened.'

'I imagine there'll be a delay to any repairs while the insurance company investigates.'

'Yeah. But it looks like Johnno was refuelling while some guys were repairing the wharf. Apparently they were using an angle grinder and it was a spark that ignited the fuel. How Johnno couldn't have noticed them working nearby is beyond everyone.'

'You, at least, are one of the lucky ones. You survived. The main thing for you now is to concentrate on getting that foot better. Easier said than done, I know, when your livelihood's up in the air. Are you all right financially in the meantime?'

'The pay's good and I've saved a fair bit. Plus, the boss has to have us covered by worker's compensation insurance so once those payments kick in I'll be OK.'

'Let the staff know if they can help you get in touch with anyone if you get stuck.'

'Thanks, Doc.'

'No problem.'

Matt headed for the door, wedging it open with his canvas sneaker. 'Oh, and, Bobby? Use the pain relief. If nothing else, it gives the nurses something to do.'

Steffi re-entered the room at that moment with Bobby's

medication and hit Matt on the arm in response to his comment. There was laughter in her eyes and a smile on her face. She seemed less tense than she had at the wharf the other day, or even yesterday at work but then, that was probably to be expected. She stepped past him, skirting around him and his sneaker-clad foot still propping the door open. He was surprised to hear himself mutter, 'It's good to have you on board.'

She looked equally surprised. 'Thanks,' she just managed to say as Matt nodded to Bobby then walked from the room, the sound of Steffi chatting to her patient fading as he let the door swing shut behind him.

Steffi felt self-conscious as she entered the cafeteria on her morning break. She'd been hoping Matt would be here and they could have a coffee together. She gave a half shrug. OK, maybe it was a bit gauche to come seeking him out like this, but it wasn't like she had a whole lot of friends just dying to catch up with her here at work. And Matt hadn't done anything other than be friendly so there was no reason he'd know her skin tingled deliciously whenever he was near. It was only natural to seek out a friendly face but it looked like he wasn't here.

The room was filled with hospital staff on their morning teabreaks but Matt definitely wasn't there and the idea of being alone in a sea of laughing, chatting people didn't appeal. She grabbed an iced coffee from the fridge and paid for it, then headed back out to the payphone in the corridor.

Her mother answered on the first ring.

'Waiting for my call?' Steffi leant against the wall, slipping one slender foot out of her shoe and rubbing it against her calf.

'No, dear, but it's nice to hear from you. Everything okay?'

'Yes, just wanted to hear how you got on at the caterer's this morning. Jess behave herself?'

'As always. Did you know the caterer is the sister of one of Lauren and Jack's colleagues?'

'Is there a less roundabout way to run that by me? Who is who and who is related to who?'

'Matt, who works at the AAS—his sister Anna is catering the wedding. She has a little girl, Susie, Jess's age.'

'I know.' At least, she'd known Matt's sister had a daughter.

'You do? So you won't mind if we get them together?'

Steffi opened her mouth to protest but her mother was on a roll. 'Because Jess is missing friends her own age and she and Susie really hit it off.'

'We'll talk about it tonight, Mum, but I'm sure it'll probably be all right.'

She ended the call and sat on a nearby bench, opening her iced coffee and taking a long drink. The fates seemed intent on linking her with Matt and part of her was eager to see what might happen. In fact, given that she'd gone in search of him herself just now, she couldn't really lay sole blame on the fates.

He was gorgeous, he did obscene things to her hormone levels and, as far as she knew, he was single. Could they just be friends? She'd never tried that before. She'd never even tried a relationship with a man before, other than with Jess's father—and that could hardly be called a great success. There were too many complicating factors in her life right now to contemplate a serious relationship, but if there was one thing the panic attacks were yelling at her it was to take some time for herself, de-stress and stop to smell the roses. Wouldn't making a friend be doing something for her?

Somewhere between the third and fourth gulps of her drink, sense returned and her long list of priorities danced before her eyes. Making new friends wasn't high up on her agenda, maybe only a few points in front of concern about how her hair looked. She stood up and fished a piece of paper and her phone card from her pocket, slipped the card into the phone and dialled the number jotted on the paper. This time it took five rings to be answered, but when she hung up, she mentally ticked off the first item on today's list.

'So you had the first attack out of the blue three months ago and you've had them on and off ever since.' Nadine, the young psychologist Lauren had recommended, was sitting cross-legged on a comfy-looking chair opposite Steffi in an office filled with pleasant scents from an aromatherapy burner and decorated with funky prints on the wall.

Steffi nodded. In her sudden moment of bravery yesterday she'd rung Nadine and been given a cancelled appointment slot for today. Then she'd started to worry she'd be told she was unbalanced, even though she knew that wasn't the case. At the beginning of her appointment she'd been squished as far into the corner of her chair as she could get but she could feel herself starting to relax now. It wasn't turning into the ordeal she'd imagined.

'I was convinced I was having a myocardial infarction.' She thought back to the terror she'd felt when she'd suddenly started having chest pain. Not to mention heart palpitations, sweating and feeling like she was being smothered. She'd been sure she was dying and had been bewildered when her symptoms had passed as quickly as they had come. By the time she'd suffered another few attacks, she'd been certain she must be extremely ill. It had taken numerous visits to her GP and multiple tests to convince her she was physically healthy and didn't have cardiac disease or something even more sinister.

Steffi described the symptoms and how she'd felt. None of what she was telling Nadine seemed to surprise her or make her think she was going crazy. Steffi relaxed and told her some more about the last few months.

'From what we've talked about, the attacks don't seem to be precipitated by anything in particular.' Steffi nodded and Nadine continued, 'That's what we call uncued, or unexpected, panic attacks.'

They started to talk about the thoughts Steffi had during her attacks. The worst was that she was suffocating or having a heart attack, even though she knew that she had no physiological medical condition. They moved onto the types of things Steffi had started to do to try and control or avoid her attacks and Nadine seemed happy when Steffi couldn't think of any, so presumably that was a good thing. Nadine was filling in a diagram as they spoke and taking notes. Steffi hoped she'd have a magic solution jotted down for her by the end of the session.

'You haven't been prescribed diazepam or something else for this?'

'No. My GP suggested using an anxiolytic but I didn't want to. I was hoping having a break from the city would make me better.'

'I spoke to your GP in Adelaide this morning, like we talked about on the phone yesterday, and although I know it's hard to go over all this again, I needed to hear it all from you and make my own diagnosis.'

'What is your diagnosis?'

'No surprises for you—panic disorder.'

'I'd rather you said I've been imagining it.'

Nadine smiled. 'It's not as bad as you think. I believe we're just looking at panic disorder. It's not co-morbid with any other condition and it's of relatively short duration so far. You've also never suffered any other mental health disorder so I'm confident of a good result in the not too distant future.' She was looking at Steffi with eyes that were kind but keen, missing nothing as she went on, 'Although much of your success will depend on your willingness to work at it.'

'I'm here now so I've got the hardest bit over and done with in my mind.' She sat up straighter in her chair. 'I'd hoped it would just stop when I came back to Port Cadney but it hasn't so I realise I need to do something about it. What *are* we going to do?' She wasn't really holding her breath for a magic solution but *any* reasonable-sounding plan of action would be like manna from heaven.

'Studies show psychological techniques have better results with panic disorder than medication, so it's perfectly OK that you hold off on that path, at least for now.' Nadine stood up and walked over to a large filing cabinet. 'I want to see you again in a week, and in the meantime…' she opened a drawer and pulled out a handout '…start on this.' She handed the notes headed 'Diary' to Steffi and explained how to keep a record of any attacks she had before their next appointment, concentrating on the thoughts she had during an attack.

'And this will help?'

'It's the first step in your treatment plan and, yes, we have good results with this particular set of techniques. Do you want me to give you another summary of what we're looking at?'

'Thanks.'

'Given your background, it's most likely the panic attacks were brought on by an acute period of stress, ex-

acerbating an already stressful life. It's not an unusual
condition, especially among women, and you're also in a
high-risk age bracket. You've already grasped the essentials of this disorder, that the physical sensations you experience are normal but you're misinterpreting them as
catastrophic, like a heart attack or imminent death, and so
you've started to focus overly on the symptoms. All of
which has made your attacks worse. Our aim is to work
to correct those misinterpretations. Make sense?'

They made an appointment for the following week and
Steffi drove home feeling a lot more upbeat than she had
for a long time. Talking to Lauren had been the first step
and now she was really feeling as if she might be back
on the right track. It was good to feel that she was taking
action to turn her life around, get her old confidence back.
And if that left her with some energy to enjoy a friendship
with Matt, maybe there'd be no harm in that. Even
Lauren's wedding was starting to gain more appeal,
whereas until today the thought of playing the happy
bridesmaid for hours had been anything but happy.

She pulled up outside her parents' house and watched
as Jess came running out to meet her. Soon the old house
would be Jack and Lauren's and her parents would have
moved to give her mother a chance to enjoy city life for
the first time in their marriage. Soon, too, Jess would grow
up and no longer run as fast as she could to hug her when
she came home. And what would her life be like then?
Life moved on, people changed, and if she didn't get her
act together now, there'd be no chance of having a full
and contented life once she no longer had a young daughter to fill her days.

She opened the door and stepped out, catching Jess in
her arms and swinging her out wide in an arc around her
body, her heart filling with joy as she saw pleasure light

up Jess's face. Steffi slowed and put her daughter back down and they held hands as they walked across the yard to the house. Little moments like these were like gold.

'Good day, sweetheart?'

'Yup. Granny and I picked up all our dresses for Saturday. Grandpa says I'll look prettier than the bride.'

Steffi smiled, feeling grateful for the umpteenth time that after a rocky start, when she'd first found out she was pregnant, her dad had been wrapped around his grand-daughter's finger from the day she'd been born. 'I bet he didn't say that with Auntie Lauren around.'

'She's at work. She's coming tonight to see our dresses on. Tomorrow's Friday, it's only two more sleeps, Mum.'

'Only two! We'd better get a wriggle on with dinner, then, or you won't be ready for Auntie Lauren.'

Matt checked his watch—a quarter past twelve. ETA was twenty-five minutes past, not long now. It seemed for ever since he and Ryan had taken off from Belcanna Station in the AAS plane, although only twenty minutes had passed.

Matt sat hunched over his seven-year-old patient, watching her intently, praying that the object she'd inhaled wouldn't dislodge more. If it moved further down Kirsten's larynx it could block her airway, suffocating her. He hadn't moved since they had picked Kirsten up from her parents' station, watching her like a hawk the whole flight.

When the call had come from Sheila, Matt hadn't ex-pected he would need to evacuate the patient. It was a common occurrence so he was frustrated that he hadn't been able to retrieve the offending object. Kirsten had cer-tainly taken a good breath in and there had been no way he could have reached the obstruction with tweezers, it was too far back.

Libby, Kirsten's mother, had tried unsuccessfully, before calling for help. It wasn't the first time he'd flown out to their place and it wouldn't be the last. The Smyth family was used to drama. With five children, each one wilder than the one before, they were familiar with all manner of childhood accidents and well known to the AAS.

Matt was concerned now but all he could do was to wait and watch and hope. If the foreign body did move and restrict her breathing, he wasn't sure what his options were in the confines of the light aircraft.

He needed to get Kirsten into Theatre. Her only chance was for him to remove it under anaesthetic. So far their luck was holding, and as long as Kirsten could continue to breathe comfortably through her mouth, they had time.

'We're approaching for landing now.' Ryan's voice drifted back from the cockpit. It had been a hectic ninety minutes since they had first left the AAS base but the episode was far from over. Matt mentally crossed his fingers that Kirsten would come through unscathed.

Connor Fitzpatrick was waiting with the ambulance to whisk Matt, Kirsten and her mum to the hospital. 'Pam asked me to let you know Theatre Two is ready for you,' the paramedic told Matt.

'Who's the anaesthetist?'

'Dave Barker. He's doing his regular Friday stint in Theatres.'

'Great. We'll take Kirsten straight to Theatre on arrival.' Matt turned to Libby. 'Pam will have a consent form prepared for you, I'll leave you to fill in all the paperwork while I fix Kirsten up, OK?'

Libby just nodded. She hadn't spoken on the flight, except to Kirsten. Matt knew she was worried but could see she was taking his instructions in.

Within fifteen minutes of landing, Connor and Matt wheeled the stretcher into the operating theatre, greeting Dave, who was already in position.

'Dr Barker is going to put a needle in the back of your hand and give you a bit of anaesthetic to make you sleepy, Kirsten. Then I'll be able to get this thing out for you,' Matt explained, before dashing off to scrub.

He returned to find the nurse, already gloved and gowned, holding a theatre gown ready for him. He slid his arms into the sleeves and did a double-take when their eyes met above her mask.

His smile was hidden by his mask but it was there in his voice as he said, 'Another one of your many talents, Steffi? Theatre nurse?'

'I'm full of surprises.'

'I don't doubt that for a minute.'

'Gloves.' She held out one and then the other for Matt to wriggle his fingers into before tying his mask.

'She's under,' Dave called out.

Matt walked over to the operating table and explained the patient's background to Dave. 'Kirsten here decided to copy her sixteen-year-old sister who's just come home with a nose ring. Unfortunately, Kirsten breathed in at the wrong time and inhaled her pretend piercing.' Matt shone a light up Kirsten's nostril to check the position of the foreign body. 'You'll need to be extremely careful when you're intubating her. I don't want to risk dislodging the foreign body. It's lodged in her larynx but too far back to reach with tweezers so I'm going to have to suction it out.'

'OK, steady as she goes.' Dave slid the artificial airway into position. 'Got it.'

'So far, so good. I need the suction unit. Tubing, please.' Matt took the thin plastic tube from Steffi and slid one end up one of Kirsten's nostrils and down the back of her larynx. His movements were slow and deliberate, not wanting to cause any unnecessary trauma to the child's airway.

'OK, I've hit a blockage.' He shone the light up Kirsten's other nostril to check his positioning. 'This must be it.' Matt switched the suction on and in less than a second had extracted a small, plastic object. Turning the suction off, he dropped the doughnut-shaped offending article into the kidney dish Steffi held out for him.

'What on earth is it?' Dave asked, glancing into the dish at the bright pink item.

Matt shrugged. 'I have no idea.'

'It's a doll's earring,' Steffi said.

'A what?' both men asked.

'An earring for a doll. It'd be the perfect size for a nose-ring for a seven-year-old.' Why did he have the feeling she was trying to stifle a laugh under her face mask?

'The things they make for kids nowadays.' Dave shook his head as he reversed the light anaesthetic.

'You mean the things we find in kids' noses,' said Steffi.

'At least it makes a change from peas,' Matt added.

'We should run a competition in the staffroom—most bizarre foreign object found shoved up a nose wins.'

'She's a lucky girl.' Steffi pulled off her mask. 'Well done, Matt.'

She slipped behind him so he couldn't see the sudden self-consciousness that had crept up on her when she'd praised him, and busied herself helping him untie his gown. Her hands brushed over his hips, sending tingles up her arms straight to her breasts. She caught her breath just in time but her fingers fumbled with the ties. She couldn't blame this strong reaction, this chemistry, on another life-threatening situation. Kirsten's incident had been potentially life-threatening but Matt's ability to perform the procedure had never been in question. There was an attraction between them, a powerful one.

Pulling apart the last of the cotton ties, she reached up to his shoulders and tugged on the green fabric, just as Matt reached one hand up to help shrug off the gown. His large hand closed over the very tips of her fingers and the sensation rocked her to the soles of her feet. He enclosed her fingers along with the fabric of the gown and slipped them both from his shoulder in one smooth movement. He loosened the fabric from her grasp but kept hold of her fingers, turning to look down at her.

She saw Matt's grey eyes darken to slate and knew he felt it, too—how could he not? It was like an electric field, like the two of them together could tap into their own private energy source. She didn't want to break the moment but there were things to be done. She looked away from him, reaching behind her, searching for the ties for her own gown.

'Let me.' Matt nodded towards the prep area, and they walked the few steps side by side. Matt took aim at the laundry bag, his gown dropping into it. He tossed his gloves and mask into the rubbish and now it was his turn to step closer and stand behind her to work at the ties of her gown.

She said nothing, just let it happen. She *wanted* this closeness with him, even if it was just to untie a couple of strings. His warm breath brushed her shoulders as he bent to help with her gown. Her hair was still tucked up into her theatre cap, leaving the soft skin of her neck exposed. Matt fumbled with the top tie and his fingers brushed the nape of her neck. This time she couldn't help it. She gasped at the contact and when he slipped the gown from her body, she twisted around to look into his eyes again and her breathing went haywire.

She felt him slip his fingers beneath the edge of her cap and pull it back off her head, felt him run his fingers over the length of her ponytail as it uncoiled, released from the cap. His hand came to rest on her shoulder, the tips of his fingers resting on her shoulder blade and the imprint of each one was as clear as though he was pressing into her skin, although his touch was light. She tilted her face up towards his, drawn to him, knowing this wasn't the time, wasn't the place, knowing she shouldn't need this, not here, not anywhere. But 'shouldn't' wasn't a word her body seemed to recognise at this moment, and her brain had gone into temporary stasis. Knowledge about what was right, what her needs were, seemed very unimportant and vaporous compared to the want that was ripping through her. She wanted him. And there wasn't a single thing she felt like doing about it. Not a single thing except standing on the tips of her toes and finding out what his lips tasted like.

CHAPTER FOUR

THE door opened and the soft sound was enough to snap them back to the real world, the world where they'd just finished in Theatre, the world where they were colleagues, nothing more.

Dave was standing half in, half out of the prep area. 'Kirsten is settled in Recovery. I'll get back to the list in Theatre One now.'

'Thanks.' Dave left and Matt cleared his throat, looking a little awkward. 'I'd better go and tell Kirsten's mum the good news. See you later?'

'At the wedding.'

He looked nonplussed. Maybe he also felt like he'd just been yanked out of a blissful dream.

'Tomorrow. Jack and Lauren's wedding.' He looked too adorable for his own good when he was confused. She'd seen him like this before, at the wharf when they first met and he'd been trying to place her.

'Sorry, my mind must have been elsewhere. No prizes for guessing where.' He tucked a strand of her hair behind her ear, the familiarity of the gesture somehow bringing to a close the strangeness of the last few minutes.

She watched as he left, running her gaze from his head, along the contours of his body, down his legs then back up again. She knew what Lauren meant about loving watching Jack walk away—she was getting the same rush from watching Matt's butt. If they hadn't been at work, she might have been hard-pressed not to haul him back in and wrap herself around him.

There was no denying that something strange was happening between them. They'd entered some personal twilight zone where sometimes she felt protected and safe and then at others…others, all she wanted to do was rip his shirt off and splay her fingers across his broad chest, which she knew instinctively would be all defined muscles and smooth brown skin. And in this space or time, whatever it was, she'd take as much as she got and there'd be no shame and no self-consciousness, only glorious worshipping of each other's bodies and minds.

Mentally, she replayed the moments since Theatre had ended. She hadn't seen it coming, and she didn't know what it meant, but a ripple of delight ran through her with the knowledge that the attraction between them was mutual. She'd worry about what it all meant later because, for the first time in a long while, she'd remembered what it was like to *not* worry and it sure felt good.

The music started to play and Steffi gave Jess a gentle nudge in the back to start her walking down the aisle. Their dresses had looked beautiful the other night, but now they'd had their hair and make-up done—even Jess had pale pink nail polish on—they all felt beautiful, too.

Steffi turned and smiled at her dad and then at Lauren, who looked stunning in a simple dress of white silk with vibrant deep red roses embroidered around the lower part of the skirt. Lauren was keyed up with excitement, not an inch of the nervous bride about her. If anything, her dad looked as if he might have trouble stopping her from sprinting down the aisle to Jack.

She turned back to watch her daughter's special moment. From the looks of it, Jess was going to make it last longer than the bride's. She was walking at a snail's pace and was only a quarter of the way down the aisle. Steffi wasn't meant to start until Jess was halfway. Maybe they'd got her so worried about going too fast that she'd gone the other way.

Steffi made an executive decision and started walking. It wouldn't do if the music stopped before Lauren had reached the altar, like musical chairs where the bride was left without a seat and was out of the game.

She took Jess's cue and decided to enjoy her brief moment in the limelight. After all, the pressure wasn't really on her, all eyes would be straining to get a look at the bride. Nonetheless, there were butterflies in her stomach and she knew she'd taken pleasure in looking her best today because Matt would be at the wedding.

She smiled to her left and right at the guests, most of whom she'd never seen before, while she wondered who it was who'd invented the 'one step, feet together' style of cruising down the aisle. She felt like a virginal maiden mincing about the gardens. Then she looked to her left, straight into Matt's appreciative eyes, and knew that the last thing she felt was virginal. There was no modesty in the heat coursing through her. If she'd been even slightly naïve, she supposed she should be blushing right now but, instead of looking shyly away, she looked dead into his eyes and sent him a killer smile. A smile that cut through the games and said, I feel it, too. I'll see you at the reception. Where had that brazenness sprung from?

He looked incredible in his dinner suit, the cut making him appear even taller and leaner than he was and the black cloth accentuating his storm-grey eyes. He'd been tugging at his bow-tie when their eyes had met and she guessed a suit was not his clothing of choice. Maybe that was jumping to conclusions, but his slightly too-long hair and the casual clothes he favoured for work seemed much more his style. The lines of his face, which might have seemed too severe framed by a more traditional cut, were softened by the waves of his dark hair touching here and there against his olive skin. And when he smiled, the angular lines of his face, with stark cheekbones and strong jaw, were transformed.

As Steffi walked to the front of the church, her mind was still full of his image. When she reached the front, Jess slipped her hand into hers and together they turned to watch Lauren, Steffi's eyes immediately searching Matt out in the congregation. It wasn't hard. He stood taller than everyone around him. As Lauren moved past him, he turned along with everyone else to watch the bride being escorted to the front of the church. Steffi looked away from him, back at Lauren, but even though she couldn't see him she was sure she could feel his eyes resting on her.

Her heart beat faster in her chest and a ripple of longing shot through her, but suddenly she was aware she was holding her breath and panic started to set in. Was she going to have an attack here right in the middle of the wedding and make a fool of herself? She took a deep breath but that seemed to make it worse. She couldn't get enough air.

As if sensing her rising panic, Lauren turned to give her the bridal bouquet and whispered, 'You're fine, Steffi. I want you to count the petals of all the flowers in my bouquet.'

Steffi looked at her, startled, as Lauren went on with the service as though nothing unusual was happening. She did as she was asked, and started counting, realising a few minutes later that the attack had been averted. As ridiculous as Lauren's order had seemed, it had taken her attention off her symptoms and the attack had passed. She chanced a glance at the congregation but no one seemed to have noticed anything. Her eyes rested on Matt and he was smiling at her. She sent him a smile in return, and it faltered a little, but at least he didn't seem to think she was an oddball. She would find out soon enough at the reception.

Steffi excused herself from the elderly relatives she'd been talking to, for ever it seemed, and made her way to the bar, feeling parched after the hours of eating and chatting.

'Lime and soda, please.' It had been a lovely evening and although the older guests were starting to leave, for the rest of them it was far from over. The dancing was only just getting under way.

Her body registered Matt's presence even before she turned around. She couldn't help the smile that appeared as she twisted slightly to look over her shoulder at him.

His voice slipped over her skin like velvet. 'Are you having as much fun as your daughter?'

'You've met?'

He nodded. 'She's a lovely child. She knows how to enjoy a party.' There was a twinkle of silver in his eyes but that was the only hint that yesterday in the prep room had ever happened.

'I know. She should have been in bed hours ago. Mum and Dad are taking her home with them when they go, so for once I don't have to be the one to ruin her fun.' She stopped herself short, almost in mid-sentence. She must be rapidly losing any points for mysterious sex appeal she'd gained in the church today, blabbing on like this.

'Are you always the one to ruin her fun? What about her dad? He must get to share that pleasure once in a while?'

'Her dad only sees her once a year or so. He—' She broke off, searching for the words to explain the odd situation she and Jess had found themselves in. 'He travels a lot with his work.'

'That must be hard.' He was looking into her eyes as if the answer mattered to him. 'For both of you.'

'Harder for Jess. She's used to it. I just wish she didn't have to be.' This conversation was surreal, further evidence they could slip seamlessly between the everyday and the sensual. 'She knows he loves her, it's just that his work takes him away.' She shrugged. 'That, and he's not really cut out for the everyday grind of parenthood. But it would do Jess good to see more of him.'

'Why have a child if he was going to leave it all to you?' He stopped. 'I'm sorry, that's really—'

'That's OK.' She bit her lip, buying time before she explained. It seemed so—sordid? stupid?—but if she wanted Matt to be her friend, perhaps it was time to be more open. If he judged her, then at least she'd know early on he wasn't the person she'd thought.

'We were young. We didn't plan on a pregnancy. To be honest, we hadn't even thought about it.' She glanced at him, gauging his response. 'I guess that's pretty obvious.'

His smile was kind, not patronising. 'It's not unusual, Steffi, it's just that a lot of people get away with not thinking. It must have been tough.' She followed his gaze across the room to where Jess was snuggled up on her grandfather's lap. 'But I can see she's a much-loved little girl.'

Steffi swallowed hard. Matt was turning out to be such a gorgeous person, inside and out. She couldn't let it affect her decision whether to return to Port Cadney, but if she *did* stay, could there be anything between them?

'You're right. I love my daughter very much.'

'You sound sad.' There was a little furrow in his brow.

'She's had a hard time lately. Picked on at school. It would've been better for both of us if Rick had been around.' For someone who played their cards close to her chest, it was unbelievable how much she was spilling to Matt. He was so easy to talk to, though, that was the problem, but if she didn't watch it, he'd have her pegged as one of those people who told their whole life story in the first five minutes of meeting someone. Actually, that was exactly what she *had* just done. 'Sorry, this is meant to be a wedding and I've been dumping all this on you. I don't normally do that.' Try ever.

He picked up her hand in his and stroked the back of it with his fingers, as if giving her this caress was the most natural thing in the world. And, to her, it seemed it was.

'You're not dumping on me, and sometimes it's easier to talk to someone you don't know so well.' He raised her hand and pressed it against his lips. It might have seemed showy but, again, it just felt *right*. There was nothing showy about Matt, he was down-to-earth. And he seemed to accept her as she was, teenage history and all.

She smiled and her heart was light. 'Then what about you? Anything you want to talk about?'

'There *is* something that's been bugging me for a while.'

She looked up at him, expectant, and was rewarded with a grin full of charm. 'Would you care to dance?'

She shook her head, laughing.

'Is that a no?'

She shook her head again, 'No, it's a yes.'

He led her to the dance floor, matching his step to hers and stopping to move a chair out of her way. The music picked up pace and he grimaced.

'Not so keen on the faster ones?'

'As long as you're not expecting Fred Astaire.'

'And here's me being such a Ginger Rogers. What a waste.' They started to move to the music, both a little self-conscious until Matt did a few particularly untalented steps and then they were laughing and it didn't matter any more that they weren't the greatest dancers. They laughed some more when, next to them, Jack spun Lauren skilfully around the floor, showing them up shamelessly. And they were still laughing over an hour later when the music had come to an end and it was time for the bride and groom to depart.

Steffi picked up her bag and followed the remaining guests outside to wave the newly-weds off. Lauren was still looking as energetic as ever but Jack was looking weary. He wrapped his arms around Steffi in a brotherly bear-hug. 'Thanks for helping make this day so wonderful for us, sister-in-law—especially for Lauren. It means the world to her to have you here.'

'And I wouldn't have missed it for the world.' She whispered in his ear, 'I hope you're not thinking of having an early night when you get to your hotel.' She nodded at Lauren. 'That one won't be needing sleep for quite some time.'

'That's what comes of cradle-snatching, I'll be forever trying to keep up with her.'

Lauren came over and bent down to hug Steffi. Everyone had to bend down to hug Steffi.

'OK, now?'

Steffi knew she was talking her near panic attack in the church. 'How did you know I needed that?'

'I was keeping an eagle eye on you in case you fell down in a dead faint and stole my thunder. Being my big sister still on the shelf, I thought you might try it.'

Steffi shook her head in mock disbelief, before giving

Lauren a kiss and squeezing her hand in silent thanks. 'Have a wonderful time, little sis.'

'We will, and thanks for everything.' She held out her hand to Jack. 'And now—' she raised her voice to the remaining guests '—my husband and I are off on our honeymoon.'

Jack added his goodbyes, and when they'd left Steffi felt bereft. As if he'd sensed it, Matt wrapped an arm around her shoulders and pulled her gently against his body. 'Can I drop you home?'

'Thanks. I'm staying at Lauren's tonight so I don't have to head back to the farm. It's not far.'

They chatted about nothing in particular on the way home and when he pulled up in front of Lauren's flat she felt surprisingly comfortable as she said, 'I've sort of had it for today so I won't ask you in for coffee, but I really did have a wonderful time this evening. Thank you.'

He unbuckled his seat belt and leant over to drop a feather-light kiss on her cheek before settling back against his seat. 'You're extremely welcome.' In the light from the streetlamp, she could see a crooked little smile on his lips. Was he feeling nervous all of a sudden?

'How about you and Jess coming for a swim some time? Susie's always at my place in the pool, and she'd love it if Jess came over. And given what you said about Jess having a hard time at school, it might be nice for her, too.' He paused and his eyes narrowed slightly. 'It's not just about Jess, though. You should know I'd like to spend time with you, too.'

'I'd also like that.' And she meant it. This time, it was Steffi who bent forward to kiss him. Buoyed by the happiness of the night and the prospect of seeing him again, she pressed her lips against his mouth and the connection was electric. It was like they'd been waiting for this moment since they'd met, or at least since yesterday. She leant into him and he slipped a hand underneath her hair to trace the line of her collar-bone. Her sigh had them both smiling at the honesty of her admission that she was attracted to him. She pulled away, and he put his hands on her shoulders, cupping his hands around her upper arms and running them slowly over her bare skin.

Her voice was breathy as she asked, 'What was that about, do you think?'

'That—' his eyes were gentle and there was laughter in them '—was the reason you didn't ask me in for coffee.' He tilted her chin up so her eyes met his. 'But now you know I'm just as dangerous in a car.'

She laughed. 'Dangerous?'

'Absolutely. Can you risk coming to my house for a swim? We'll be in bathers, with lots of warm water to play in—'

'And two eight-year-old chaperones. Yes, I think I can risk it.'

He chucked her under the chin and laughed. 'Fancy catching up for a coffee at work this week and sorting out the details?'

She nodded before saying goodbye. She was sorry he didn't kiss her again but he rumpled her hair as if she meant something to him, and when she snuggled into bed a short while later she mulled over what it all might come to mean. He wanted to see her again. He seemed to like Jess. And she was getting her life sorted out. Maybe this could go somewhere, maybe not, but for the first time in her adult life she'd made a real connection with a man. It had happened without her even really being aware of it and now it seemed as if they'd known each other for much longer than a total of about what? Eighteen hours, all up?

She crossed her fingers under her pillow and hoped that,

whatever happened, it would last longer than a swim at his place.

Steffi came into the ward and saw Sarah Fitzpatrick, the physiotherapist, at Bobby's bed.

'How about standing first and seeing how you go? It's not going to be as easy as you think,' she was saying to the young fisherman. 'Can you give me a hand, Steffi? Bobby is ready to try standing today, although he thinks he's ready to walk.' Steffi and Sarah exchanged a smile. 'Hospital policy says it must be a two-person assist.'

'Sure. Where do you want me?'

'Stand on his right side, I'll take his injured side.'

Sarah placed the crutches within arm's reach against the wall and moved the visitor's chair and bedside cabinet out of the way to create some extra space.

'OK, sit on the edge of the bed for me.' To Steffi she added, 'Bobby has been practising sitting on the edge of the bed with his foot hanging down.'

Steffi knew the biggest hurdle for bedridden patients on their first attempt at getting out of bed was usually light-headedness caused by moving from a horizontal position to a vertical one. For Bobby, the rush of blood to his fractured ankle, which was used to being elevated, would also be an uncomfortable sensation and so Sarah had tried to minimise the difficulty by having him practise being semi-upright.

'Are you OK to support him under one arm as he stands?'

Steffi nodded.

'Right, then, Bobby, I want you to push off the bed and stand on your right foot. Keep your left foot off the ground for now.' Bobby stood up as Steffi and Sarah braced themselves to take the sudden weight, supporting him at either side.

Steffi watched the colour in his face. So far so good.

'Try touching your left toes onto the floor. That's all you have to do today. Pull your bottom in,' Sarah said as Bobby started to sag at the hips. 'It helps you to stand tall. That's the way. Do you want to try standing with the crutches?'

Steffi knew Sarah must be happy with both his balance and colour to suggest the crutches.

'I think so.'

Sarah passed one crutch to Steffi and then tucked the second one under Bobby's left armpit. 'Let's see if I measured you correctly.' She checked the height of the hand-rests and the gap between the arm-rests and Bobby's armpits. 'Perfect, as long as you stand tall. OK, Steffi, hands off.'

Bobby stood quite steadily. Sarah remained close, ready to help him back to his bed if he started to falter. She let him stand for a minute before calling it a day.

'Well done. Lift your left foot off the floor and let go of your right crutch. Good, now reach behind you—can you feel the bed?'

He nodded.

'Bend your right knee and sit back down on the bed. Terrific. I'll help you swing your legs up. How do you feel?'

'Worn out.'

'You didn't believe me when I said it would knock the stuffing out of you, did you?'

'I still can't believe it was that much effort.'

'Men aren't as tough as they like to think they are,' Sarah teased.

Sarah and Steffi laughed as Bobby pulled a face.

'No comeback even?' Steffi asked.

'Picking on my patient?'

A faint veil of heat crept over Steffi's cheeks at the sound of Matt's voice. She took a deep breath and turned to look at him, leaning against the doorframe. She hadn't seen him since he'd dropped her at Lauren's after the wedding. Since he'd suggested coffee and a swim. The heat in her cheeks intensified as she pictured him wearing not much at all, droplets of water running over his brown skin.

Sarah fired her response back. 'Absolutely.'

'It's OK, Doc, I can handle it.'

'Sounds like you'll have to.' He straightened up and asked, 'Do you have a minute before your next patient?'

Steffi's heart sank. The invitation hadn't been for her.

'Sure.' Sarah nodded. 'Just give me a sec to go through Bobby's instructions with him again.'

Steffi and Matt took their cue to leave, Matt holding the door open for her on their way out, holding her lightly by the arm and stepping to the side of the corridor, where they'd be out of the way of other staff.

'I've missed you the last few days. I've only had time to dash in and out of here first thing in the morning and last thing at night to see my patients.'

'Busy on call?'

He nodded. 'Have you got time for that coffee? It won't just be us, but I've learnt to take a break when I can. I'm on call again so there's no telling how long I'll have.'

'I'd like that.'

Sarah came out and they fell into step.

'I hope we're "consulting" over coffee.'

'You know me too well.'

Sarah laughed and, as they entered the cafeteria and Matt headed off to order their drinks, said in an aside to

Steffi, 'Overstatement of the year. He's a closed book, our Matt.'

Steffi checked where he was and saw him leaning on the counter, waiting for their hot drinks. They had a few minutes to talk. 'How long have you known him?'

'Three years, since he came to Port Cadney. He's done the unthinkable in the country and managed to keep his private life to himself. I know he has a sister here, and a niece, that he's a great doctor and always has a kind word for everyone.' She laughed. 'Not to mention that he's rather easy on the eye. *That* hasn't escaped the notice of the single women here.'

'Has he dated anyone?'

'No. The hospital grapevine would make sure we knew about it.'

'Knew about what?' He was back.

Steffi's heart leapt into her mouth at the thought that Sarah might tell him, but she was more discreet than that. 'Women's talk. What did you want to talk about?'

'Do you still do community health work?'

'Yes, a few half-days a week. Why?'

'Alex Carter is ready to be discharged but his living arrangements aren't ideal. He shares a house with two other young guys, and while I don't think he'll be tempted to overdo any housework I'm still a bit concerned about how he'll manage with his arm in that sling. I'd like to refer him to you for home visits, have someone keep an eye on him.'

'I can certainly add him to my list and check his exercises. Do you want him put on the home nursing list as well? It might be a good idea for showering and things like that.'

'Sounds good to me.'

'OK. I'll fill in the request forms and get you to sign them.'

'Tell me more about community health work,' Steffi said.

'We provide home care to people who don't require hospitalisation but aren't able to manage on their own. Physio, nursing, occupational therapy or a combination, either short or long term.'

'How many nurses do you employ?'

'Never enough. The usual story. Why? Are you interested in working with us?'

'Actually, I might be.'

Sarah wrote down her number for Steffi, handing the paper to her and saying, 'I'm working there tomorrow so you could come and tag along if you like. If you're still interested then, I'll set you up with an interview. The director is always keen to find more nurses.' She drained the last of her coffee. 'I have to get going, but give me a call tonight if you want to come.'

'I'd love to but I'm filling in for an AAS clinic run tomorrow. Can I arrange a different time with you?'

'Sure. It's probably better if you went with one of the nurses anyway, to give you a better idea of the work involved. Any time you're free would suit.'

'More surprises?' Matt asked as Sarah departed.

'Pardon?'

'The clinic run. You're filling in?'

'Yes. With Lauren away and Chloe in Adelaide on a refresher course for a week, the AAS is short-staffed, too. I'm not qualified to fill in for any on-call work but the clinics are no problem. I'm only needed for a couple.'

'I'm on the clinic run tomorrow.'

'Is that OK with you, me coming?'

'I'll look forward to it.' His grey eyes were shining.

'Just the two of us in a small plane, thrown together for several hours...' His voice trailed off.

'You forgot the pilot.'

'I know.'

She sobered up as a thought occurred to her. 'Just how small is "small"?'

'Worried?'

'No.' She paused. 'Maybe.'

He raised one eyebrow.

'I'm sticking with "maybe"'

'We'll find out soon enough.'

Steffi and Matt were buckled into their seats in the state-of-the-art Pilatus PC-12. As Matt had predicted, they were alone, other than their pilot, Ryan Fitzpatrick. Beside them there were two stretchers and one empty seat, all inter-changeable depending on need.

'When you said small, you meant pretty jolly tiny, didn't you?'

'Has that "maybe" become a definite "yes"? You're worried?'

'No.'

'You're as stubborn as your sister. How about I fill you in on our schedule, as much as we have one. That'll help you forget all your worries. The clinic in Ceduna is pretty new on our list. It's been going for about two months and today we're conducting a child and infant health clinic.'

'Why is a clinic needed there? I thought Ceduna had its own GP and hospital?'

'It does. But the GP gets pretty snowed under and there's been a big publicity campaign on immunisation recently. Once the campaign stops most people forget about how important immunisation is, and if it's difficult to see a health professional they just let it go. We need to catch the parents while it's fresh in their minds.'

'Is that all we're doing today, immunisations?'

'No. All the other regular paediatric assessments, too. Age-related health checks, for babies and pre-schoolers, eye and chest exams, and there are usually a few mums who want to be seen as well. Often they've driven in from one hundred kilometres or more away and they're not going to make that trip twice for a medical check so we see them, too.'

Steffi glanced out of the window as she listened to Matt, and the view momentarily stunned her. They were nearing Ceduna now and on their left was the start of the Great Australian Bight. Massive cliffs dropped away to the ocean in one bay and then wide, white sandy beaches stretched for miles in the next. The water was bright blue close to shore, darkening to black as it deepened. The contrast of colours between the red desert sands on their right and the white beach sands on their left was startling.

'Magnificent, isn't it?'

Steffi turned to him, her face alight with pleasure. 'I've never flown over this part of the country before. It's so beautiful.'

For a brief moment Matt wished he were a man who was comfortable with expressing his feelings. Steffi's eyes were the same blue as the sea and as breath-taking, but he couldn't bring himself to say anything before the chance was gone.

'Starting our descent now.' Ryan's voice came through the intercom and Matt and Steffi were thrust back into work mode.

They were met at the airport by the president of the local branch of the Country Women's Association who drove them to the hospital.

Matt commented, 'That's one bonus about Ceduna. Apart from the incredible scenery, we actually have a well set-up facility. Some of the clinics operate out of the local hall but, even then, the CWA do a fantastic job. There're always toys for the kids and lunch is provided for us.'

From the minute the clinic started at ten o'clock until the lunch-break at midday, they scarcely drew breath. The appointment schedule was kept running relatively smoothly by one of the hospital admin staff, but the minute Steffi said goodbye to one patient there was another waiting to take her place.

When she wasn't doing immunisations and weighing and measuring children, she was assisting Matt when he was treating any of the mothers. Some wanted cervical screening examinations and others simply needed skin checks for any suspicious moles or blemishes. Skin cancer was a very real danger in the outback.

Lunch was only a quick break but the hospital kitchen had prepared a delicious assortment of sandwiches, cakes and fresh fruit.

'I could get used to this,' Steffi said as she made her selection.

'They like to keep us well fed and I'm certainly not complaining,' Matt said as he piled his plate high with food. Steffi wondered where it all went. He didn't have an ounce of excess flesh on his frame. 'Can I get you a drink?'

'I'd love a cup of tea and a huge glass of water. I haven't talked so much in a long time. I'm parched.'

'So many of our patients live in such isolation that we're the only people they'll see for weeks at a time. They need the social contact from us as much as they need our expertise.' The corners of his eyes creased up as he smiled, lines running around his mouth, too, all telling a story about him. And most of all telling her he was real. Genuine. 'Drinks coming up.'

CHAPTER FIVE

SHORTLY after taking off from Ceduna airport, Matt's attention was caught when Ryan's voice came through the intercom system. 'Matt, we're being diverted. Fractured leg at Buckleboo Station—Don Douglas.'

Matt headed for the cockpit and slipped on the headphones before Ryan told Sheila to continue.

'He's on his own at the property. He was fixing one of the cars and the jack collapsed and broke his leg. There's an airstrip on the property. Co-ordinates 32°S, 136°E.'

Ryan checked the global positioning system. 'We're about due north of Wudinna at the moment so our ETA would be about ten minutes. What condition is the airstrip in?'

'Good, apparently, but it's about one and a half k's from the house so Matt will have to make his own way there.'

'OK. I'll let you know when we're about to land. Over and out.'

Matt made his way back to Steffi and explained the situation. 'Happy to give me a hand? It's just like A and E work, only out in the bush. It does happen sometimes that we get diverted if we're closer than the on-call team.'

'What should I expect?'

'Don reckons he's fractured his leg. Didn't say whether it was upper or lower, but either way we'll need to stabilise him and then evacuate. Usual nursing procedure—obs, fluid, pain relief. The drawback is he's on his own at the station and it's a bit of a hike from the airstrip.'

'Can Ryan radio the base and ask Sheila to let Mum and Dad know I'll be late back?'

'Sure thing.' He straightened up to head back to the cockpit but stopped as he realised she wasn't looking too ecstatic about the change of plans, although she seemed to be doing her best not to show she was apprehensive. 'It'll be fine, Steffi. No need to worry.'

There wasn't much more he could do, he was needed to act as copilot to Ryan for landing, but he walked away with the uneasy feeling that he'd like to have made her troubles disappear. Which just wasn't possible. At the end of the day, no one could do that for another person.

Within a short while, they were flying over the property. Ryan made one pass low over the airstrip while Matt kept his eyes peeled for anything untoward. 'It's a bit hard to tell what's what with all these daisies growing everywhere. I think Don needs to graze some of his sheep on the strip.'

'I don't need to remind you, Matt, sheep and airstrips are a dangerous combination.'

Matt chuckled. Not so long ago Ryan had tangled with an errant sheep on a landing strip, wiping out one side of his plane in the process. 'I can't see anything too large poking through the flowers. And no woolly animals.'

'OK. Let's give it a whirl.' Ryan touched down without incident but pulled the plane up as quickly as possible, not wanting to give disaster more time than necessary to strike his precious aircraft.

Matt jumped out as soon as the plane had stopped and took off across the paddock, heading west towards the house. He carried a sphygmomanometer and some pressure bandages with him, the bare essentials, planning on returning for his team and full supplies. His long legs soon had him looking like a speck in the distance but it was a seemingly interminable eighteen and a half minutes before he reappeared driving a beaten-up farm truck. Steffi had checked her watch every thirty seconds in between trying to remember what equipment Matt had asked for and finding where it was stored in the aircraft. Ryan had kept busy checking over every inch of the airstrip, wanting to ensure it would be safe to take off again.

They both looked at the truck in disbelief when Matt pulled up alongside the plane. The driver's side door was missing, it had no windscreen and the back of the truck was a flatbed fitted with a huge stock crate.

'Is that the best you could do?' Steffi asked. She couldn't imagine riding in such a rough vehicle, let alone transporting an injured person in it.

'Come on, Stef, you've seen Matt's car. He's only comfortable with cars that should have been retired years ago. We'll get to the house and there'll be a brand-new ute sitting there with the keys in it and Matt will have chosen this one on purpose.'

'Ha. Ha. This was all there was, if you don't count the car that Don was working on, which is now leaking oil all over the ground. I've come to collect the equipment. You're more than welcome to walk back if you don't want to share my wheels.'

'Since you put it that way…' Ryan started to stack things into the back of the truck as Matt handed them to him, the medical kit and bags of fluid followed by an inflatable mattress and leg splint.

'Hop in front, Steffi,' Ryan instructed as he jumped into the back.

Matt drove quickly over the rough dirt road back to the house.

'Don's inside. He's fractured his right femur, but otherwise seemed pretty right,' he said as he leapt out of the cab, grabbing the medical kit before heading for the house. 'Bring the fluid.'

Inside, Matt took charge. 'Don, this is Steffi Harrison, she's a nurse. This big bloke over here is Ryan Fitzpatrick, he's our pilot and part-time orderly. Take his obs again for me, please, Steffi. His BP was 105 over 70 before, pulse 140.'

Steffi knew Matt would have checked Don's vital signs initially to ensure he wasn't bleeding internally before returning to the plane. She repeated the obs as Matt inserted a bung into the back of Don's hand and set up an IV line to run fluids.

'Ryan, can you fold the vacuum mattress out and inflate it using the foot pump?'

'Pulse 130, BP 110 over 70.'

'Right. Don, I'm going to pop this splint on to your leg to help keep it still while we're transferring you, and I'll give you something for the pain.' Matt slid the rubber splint under Don's leg from heel to groin, fastening it at the front. 'Steffi, can you inflate it for me? Just squeeze this pump until the splint is firm around Don's leg.' He handed the small hand valve to Steffi and rummaged through the medical kit for the morphine, drawing up the correct dose and administering it through Don's IV line.

'OK, how are we doing?'

'Mattress is done.'

'I'm done, too.'

'Don, we're going to get you out to the plane now as gently as we can. Steffi, while Ryan and I lift, can you slide the mattress under him?'

She nodded.

'Ryan, I'll take Don's legs, you take his trunk. On the count of three.' Matt looked at both his coworkers, both in half-kneeling positions on either side of their patient, and they nodded their agreement. 'One, two, three.'

Matt and Ryan lifted Don off the floor and Steffi slid the mattress under him from the other side. As soon as it was in position the men lowered Don onto the makeshift stretcher.

'Ryan and I will take the top and bottom, you stay alongside to steady it, Steffi.'

Together they somehow managed to load Don into the back of the truck. It wasn't the most hygienic ambulance but it would do the job. Steffi was grateful the fracture hadn't been a compound one. He would undoubtedly have picked up an infection in these conditions if he'd had an open wound.

Steffi and Ryan collected the equipment and, with Matt taking the open-air seat this time, Ryan drove slowly back to the airstrip, trying not to jolt their patient around unnecessarily.

At the airstrip Don was transferred to the plane's stretcher and lifted into the aircraft by the mechanical hoist. The morphine had given him some relief and he was half-asleep now. Matt checked his obs again as Ryan prepared for take-off and Steffi collapsed into her seat.

'Are you OK?' Matt reached across, touching her hand for a brief moment.

'That was incredible.' Her heart was racing. Adrenalin from the retrieval or was it because of Matt? 'You were incredible.'

'You weren't too bad yourself.'

'I'm a mess. I was a bundle of nerves and all I had to do was hold this and count that. You were so in control.'

'This type of thing is my favourite part of the job.'

'Tell me what you like about it.' Steffi knew she had a captive audience for the next hour, barring any further problems with their patient who was now asleep. It might be her chance to find out more about this man who had her tied up in emotional knots.

At the request, Matt settled back in his seat, a grin on his face, as if just thinking about his job was enough to set everything right in his world. 'I love the unexpected nature of the work, the fact that I have to think on my feet and I come across all sorts of things I've never seen in a textbook and am never likely to. I love that I have to make quick decisions, quick but well-informed ones.'

'Don't you find it stressful?'

A little crease appeared between his eyes as he thought about her question. 'I've never felt stressed. Even the smallest thing I can do is better than nothing. It's challenging. And rewarding.'

'Lauren loves it, too. I don't think I could handle the responsibility of things being completely in my hands.'

'It's not so different to the responsibility of being a single parent. You make decisions affecting Jess every day and you do that on your own.'

'But hopefully not decisions that might mean the difference between life and death.'

'Maybe not. But they're big decisions all the same and you learn to make them and you make them to the best of your ability.'

'Mmm.' Her abilities had been less than terrific lately but she didn't want to discuss her failings right now. She ignored a twinge of guilt that she hadn't confided in Matt about her panic attacks and that now might be the perfect time. But he seemed to have such a high opinion of how she coped with motherhood, with her work, and she knew she wanted to bask in the glow of his good opinion for a while longer. Beside, he'd never said much about himself, and now was also a perfect opportunity for that. She wanted to talk about him for a change. Gorgeous, heart-melting him. Mentally, she ground her heel into the last of her guilt over not confiding in him, letting him think the best of her, at least for now. 'How long have you worked with the AAS?'

'A bit over three years now.'

'How did you end up here?'

'I grew up in the country.'

'Really?' No one had mentioned that to her. 'Where?'

'Not far from here. But I went to boarding school in Adelaide when I was twelve. I decided when I was about fifteen I wanted to be a doctor and I've never wavered from that.'

'Did you know then that you wanted to join the AAS?'

'Not specifically, but once I started university most branches of medicine didn't appeal to me. I think perhaps I wasn't really cut out for those that the ''old school,'' for want of a better term, hold in high regard. Being a specialist in the city wasn't my idea of medicine but I loved the AAS from day one of my first placement. I like the autonomy and remoteness and I don't miss out on ''real'' medicine.'

'You seemed so comfortable out there, even though I wouldn't have thought it a relaxed situation.' She was a bit envious of how calm he'd been. Emergency medicine had never been her thing, even before her panic disorder had set in.

'You grew up here, too—you know how relaxed the lifestyle is.'

'I'm not talking about the lifestyle, I'm talking about your work.'

'All part of the same thing. I love getting out on the plane and I'll do it until the day I retire. Can't think of anything worse than to be stuck indoors in a hospital or general practice.'

'But you do hospital work, too.'

'I do hospital work because it's part of my job description, but I really would rather not have to.'

'That's where we differ, then. I like to know what I'm going to be dealing with. And I like to know where I'm going to be working. I need a familiar environment.'

'Maybe it's because you've had to provide for someone else. You've always had Jess's well-being to consider.'

Would she, could she, have been more adaptable, spontaneous, under different circumstances? She doubted it. She shook her head. 'I think I was like that anyway. Why, do you think you'd change if you had someone else to consider?'

'As long as I knew I could provide for them, I know I'd always prefer to stay out of mainstream work. That's just who I am.' He glanced out of the window, then at his watch. 'We're nearly home now. How about that swim we've talked about? I could use a refreshing dip once Don is sorted at the hospital.'

Steffi had so many more questions for him but he suddenly seemed to have run out of answers. He certainly did a very neat change of topic and she let it go. She knew far more about him now than she had before this flight. She'd have to be content with that. 'Can I take a raincheck? I'd love to say yes but I really need to get home to Jess.'

'Saturday?'

'That would be perfect.'

Once their plane landed at Port Cadney airport Matt was swept up in a bustle of activity revolving around transferring Don to the ambulance and sorting out the equipment, supplies and paperwork. She had no chance to do more than wave goodbye from a distance, but her heart soared as he caught her eye and grinned at her before turning back to his patient. Saturday would come soon enough. She could wait.

'Jess, hurry *up*, we're going to be late.'

'But I can't find my pink hat.'

'Leave it, I've already got your green one.'

'But I need my pink one!'

Steffi gritted her teeth and sprinted into Jess's room, jumping over piles of discarded clothes and lifting item after item in search of the hat.

She found it in a pile Jess had already apparently looked through and started to say something about looking properly—but what was the point? 'Got everything else?'

Jess patted her beach-bag. 'Yup. Let's go. Race you to the car.'

Twenty minutes later, Steffi slowed down to turn into Matt's street and started to look for the street numbers. Twenty-eight, thirty, thirty-two. This was it, an old double-fronted sandstone cottage, full of charm and character and in need of a good lick of paint. She turned into the driveway and parked behind Matt's car, Jess jumping out and racing to the house even before Steffi had cut the engine.

Jess had dumped her bag on the front verandah and was knocking on the door, only a notch down from hammering. At least she'd break the ice, if not the door knocker, for them both.

The door flew open. 'Come and see my new dog.' And Jess disappeared in a whirl of pink and purple. Steffi assumed the purple-wearing child had been Matt's niece, Susie.

Behind them, Matt was lounging against the doorframe,

his hands in the pockets of his board shorts. 'I don't have a new dog, but would you like to come in anyway?' He unfolded himself and took a step towards Steffi, stretching a hand out, placing it at her elbow and welcoming her inside, taking her beach-bag in his other hand.

She leant in towards him, feeling the strength of his body, liking the feel of his large hand on her elbow, breathing in the sandalwood scent of him as they walked down the cool hallway.

'Does Susie really have a dog?'

He laughed. 'She wouldn't know what to do with a real one, the novelty would wear off inside a week. It's one of those battery-operated gizmos that "communicates" with you.' Matt opened a door that took them into the family and kitchen area at the back of the house.

'Great, now I'll have Jess nagging me for one.' She stopped and looked about. 'This is lovely.' The back wall was floor-to-ceiling glass with doors opening onto a shaded paved area, beyond which the pool glittered and sparkled in the sun. 'Did you do the renovation?'

'I managed the site and contracted all the workers, and I did a fair bit of it myself.'

'Like what?'

'The timberwork, windows, kitchen.'

Steffi's jaw dropped as she took in the kitchen, made of pale, limed wood, with gorgeous old tiles on the splashbacks, understated, simple, but one hundred per cent good taste.

'I'm impressed.'

'Don't be, it's something I've done for years. I like working with wood, enjoy making things. If I hadn't done medicine I would probably have been a carpenter.' He slipped his hands into his pockets again, and half sat on the edge of the solid kitchen table. 'And I couldn't afford to have someone else make it for me.'

'I know the feeling, but unfortunately my creative talents only stretch to sewing costumes for school plays, and even that I do badly.' She shuddered at the thought of Jess's sulky face when she saw Steffi's attempts at her costumes. 'And unwillingly.'

'Bad memories?'

'Shocking.'

'Then you enjoy sewing as much as I enjoy painting.' He waved a hand in the direction of the original front part of the house. 'My sister's always on at me to finish the job but...'

'It doesn't light your fire?'

'Frankly, no.' They smiled, relaxing in each other's company. 'Can I get you a drink?'

'Water would be great. I'd forgotten how much hotter it is here than Adelaide.'

She followed Matt and perched at the breakfast bar. A framed photo, perched next to a collection of cookbooks, caught her eye.

'Are they your parents?'

Matt's eyes flicked up from the glass he was filling. 'Mmm.' He returned his attention to the task at hand.

'Do they live nearby?'

'No.' He continued to fill the second glass, not bothering to look up this time. Surely pouring water didn't require his total concentration?

'You've got your father's eyes.'

No comment at all this time.

Not one that was relevant anyway.

'How would you feel if we took the girls to the beach instead of staying here?' He gestured outside. 'The Cove would be perfect today. There's no wind and it might be the last day we get to use the sea this autumn.'

'Fine by me. Jess will love it. Can we drag them away from that dog?'

'Absolutely. If nothing else, Susie knows she can always wheedle an ice cream out of me after the beach.'

'You're telling me you're a big old softy?'

He raised one eyebrow. 'My lips are sealed.'

'A man of mystery. Intriguing.'

'Last one in is a rotten egg,' squealed Susie, running for the water as fast as her little legs would take her, Jess in hot pursuit.

Matt was standing next to Steffi, his feet apart and hands on his hips, bare above his board shorts. He looked at her with a twinkle in his eye. 'It's only fair to give them a head start,' he said, before he took off after them, kicking the white sand up with his heels as he ran, his smooth back rippling with muscles. The sight of him held Steffi transfixed.

He caught up to the girls just as they reached the water and, barely slowing, picked one up under each arm and kept running into the water, great arcs of it splashing up around them, little girl-squeals of excitement ringing out and probably half deafening him.

It was another side to him entirely, carefree, fun, spontaneous. She licked her lips and sank to the ground to sit on her beach towel. Get your breath back, get your breath back.

At least this breathlessness wasn't due to the panic attacks. She hadn't had any since she'd averted the one at the wedding. She'd thought she'd been on to a quick cure then, but Nadine had explained that distraction wasn't a method she could rely on. What had she said? Distraction would distract her from her anxiety but she'd also become distracted from everything else around her. She'd be switched off.

She slipped her sunglasses off, the shade of her hat sufficient. Matt was now crouched down just beyond the breakers, out in deeper water, and each girl was taking a turn to climb onto him, putting one foot in his cupped hands, before he launched her to land with a splash.

Steffi looked away from them at their surroundings, seeing the cliffs forming a natural enclosure to the beach at either end, the white sand ending against a jumble of reddish rocks heaped in piles, rising to blend with the walls of red rock. The water was a clear blue-green, and she knew from the clifftop it would be very clear and wouldn't darken to deep blue until a good hundred metres out from shore. The waves were small, not even enough to body-surf in, but perfect for two little girls to enjoy.

Her attention was caught by a bright pink suntop and she lifted her hat a little higher so she could watch Jess. Susie had just swum out of the way after being thrown by Matt and it was Jess's turn now. She was climbing up, her face wreathed in smiles, twisting to wave at Steffi as if she didn't have a care in the world. When had she last looked quite like that? Quite so happy?

She flipped around again in Matt's arms, calling over her shoulder, 'Watch me, Mum.' Matt flexed his arms and sent her flying into the water, her head coming up seconds later. She was screaming with laughter. 'Did you see? Did you see?'

'I saw, sweetheart.' She was laughing, too, Jess's gaiety infectious.

'Come in, Mum!'

'In a minute.'

'Make her, Matt, go get her.' Susie and Jess were hanging off him like two little monkeys.

Matt stood up in the water, the water and the girls slipping off him. 'Do I need to take such drastic measures?' The mock seriousness of his voice had Jess and Susie clapping and screaming in expectation of an adult-sized dunking.

Yes, please. But she said, 'No, I think I can manage.' She stood up and slipped off her bright sarong and hat, revealing a fuschia-coloured swimsuit, cut low in front with thin straps. As she walked to the sea, she wondered whether Matt thought he'd landed in a world where the only colour was pink. If men even noticed things like that. Did they?

They did.

'Pink suits you.'

She was wading as elegantly as she could through the water.

'Thanks.'

'Water suits you.'

Steffi had a single second to look bemused before, 'Ah-h! It's cold!' she spluttered as he brought her back above the water.

He'd dunked her unceremoniously, without warning, given her a huge dunking, scooping her up and plunging them both under the water, his lean, well-defined arms wrapping around her almost naked flesh.

And when he brought her back up, he didn't let go, slipping his hands to her waist while cries of, 'Do it again! Do it again,' floated around them.

'Why don't you two monkeys go get your beach-ball and we'll play water-catch?'

Four little legs scrambled out of the sea, thumping back

up to their towels and the mounds of buckets and spades and balls.

Steffi scraped her sodden hair back from her face—so much for actually making an effort with her appearance. Whereas Matt couldn't possibly look any hotter than he did right now, wet hair, glistening, damp skin, making him seem even browner and sleeker, polished almost, like satin. He smiled, his white teeth a stark contrast to his tanned face and, with the sun shining directly on him, he squinted against the light, the lines around his mouth and eyes softening. He spun them both around so they could look at each other without fighting the sun, and her eyes flew straight to his mouth, remembering. She parted her lips, a tiny sigh coming from her, and reached her hands out to place them on his shoulders, feeling the rock-hard ridges of bone and muscle beneath her fingers.

'You make it damnably hard not to kiss you, Steffi Harrison.'

'You make it damnably hard not to let you.'

He brought her closer, their bodies almost touching under the warm water, the salty tang in their mouths and filling their nostrils, fighting the urge to press against each other, skin against skin, mouth against mouth.

She saw him swallow and heard a soft groan escape his lips. She knew that if she pressed closer she would feel his arousal, knew their feelings were in sync. But she stayed where she was, she couldn't risk moving nearer. One of her bather straps had slipped down and he eased it back into place before taking a step away.

'Later?' It was only one word but they both knew what it meant.

'Yes.' Her answer shot back, surprising her with its huskiness and its speed.

'Come and build something with us!'

Steffi jumped at the plea and Matt waved at the girls, laden with beach gear, struggling towards the water.

'Looks like we're back on.' He chuckled as Jess dropped an armful and struggled to pick it up again. 'They couldn't possibly make two trips.'

By the time an hour had passed, the side view of an enormous camper van had been constructed out of sand, complete with curtains of seaweed and a string of shells hanging from its rear-view mirror.

Steffi dusted off her hands and sat back on her heels, pulling her sarong into place. 'That's nothing short of a miracle.'

'Uncle Matt and I have made way better things. We even made a sculpture of ourselves this summer and it looked exactly like us.'

'Cool!' Jess seemed to think that summed it up. 'Let's be dolphins.' And they were off again, back into the water. Matt and Steffi stood up, too, and walked to the water's edge, where the tiny waves that had made it this far lapped about their ankles.

'I'd forgotten how lovely it is here.'

'The Cove?'

She nodded. 'And the town, the people, the lifestyle.'

'Tired of the city lights?'

'I think I was tired of them by the time I'd unpacked all those years ago.'

'Then why stay? Especially when you'd just had a baby. Why make it so hard?'

Something in his voice made her think he knew more than she'd told him before but, then, this was the country, and he worked with her sister and brother-in-law. 'You've been talking to Lauren?'

'Not specifically, but I do remember her and Jack having arguments about single mothers when he first got here and how angry she'd get with him. Ryan told me why it pushed her buttons, why she's so involved in her teenage mothers' groups now.'

'It made quite an impression on her, I know. She was only sixteen at the time, ready to right the wrongs of the world. Still is.'

'So why go?' He wasn't going to drop the subject, she could see that.

Matt watched as she circled her toes in the sand, the patterns forming before disappearing in the water.

'I had to prove I could make it on my own. I was stubborn. Naïve. I had no idea how hard it would be to relocate. And I didn't really think I'd be left alone to raise a baby. I thought Jess's father might stay around.'

'Where is he now?'

'Saudi Arabia, I think. We communicate via email so I haven't really paid attention. It's pointless trying to keep track of him, he's a bit of a wanderer. I realised early on I'd have to support the two of us and I needed a career. I had to be in the city to study nursing. If I'd come home then I wouldn't have my qualifications.'

'Your family didn't help?'

'As much as they could. Mum and Lauren would come down for visits, Mum and Dad helped me out financially when they could, and they probably would have done more if I hadn't been so bloody-minded about being independent. Jess's dad sent a bit now and then, but he's never been what you'd call a regular worker and at the time he was so young.' She paused for a moment and Matt sensed she was back in a past that didn't include him. 'Besides, at the end of the day, I'm glad I showed myself I could do it.'

'And now?' He followed her gaze out to the girls, diving under the water over and over again, arms against their sides, feet and legs flipping madly under the water, still pretending to be dolphins.

'Now?' She linked her hands and stretched her slender arms out in front of her. 'Now I'm thinking it might be time to come home.'

A knot appeared in his stomach. 'Why?'

'Lots of reasons. Not least of which is Jess.' She caught her sarong and held it against her thighs as a sudden gust of wind whipped up and died down just as quickly. 'She's the most important person in my life and I need to do what's right for both of us. Remember I said she was being bullied? I didn't find out about it until near the end of term. I need to reassess our lives in the city. I'm not prepared to sacrifice the relationship with my daughter for the sake of my job.'

Peals of laughter floated towards them and a sudden smile swept across Steffi's face. Matt saw it, and it was like the sun coming out. Her voice was bright as she said, 'And it's been a long time since she's been this happy, being back here.'

'You're feeling guilty you didn't know about it sooner?'

'Of course. And angry at the school for not picking up on it and alerting me.'

'Children are masters at hiding things. If Jess didn't want you to know, chances are, you weren't going to find out.'

'She's only eight!'

'I know, I'm just saying you won't always know everything, no matter how close you are.'

'How would you know?' She must have seen his surprise as she dropped her voice immediately. 'Sorry.'

'It's OK. You're right, I'm not a parent but I do know that I kept a lot of things that happened at boarding school quiet. My folks certainly didn't hear about everything that went on. Not half of it.'

'What did you keep from them?'

'Things they could do nothing about.'

'But they'd have wanted to know about any problems you were having. I'd do anything for Jess.'

'It doesn't matter. What's the point in complaining to people about things that are out of their control, things no one can do anything about? Dad made that clear when I did try to tell him about a few things, and after that I didn't try. He was right. I could see it was my battle.' He held up a hand to silence Steffi, who looked like she was about to protest that that hadn't been the situation with Jess. 'I'm not saying the two are the same, my point is how easy it is to keep things hidden.'

'But you were at boarding school. I see Jess every day and I still didn't know.'

'Maybe she didn't want to upset you. Kids are very perceptive. Perhaps she knew you had other worries.'

'Are you saying an eight-year-old should be able to cope on their own?'

'No, not that they should, just that they might feel they need to, that it's their problem and no one else can help.'

'You're saying that's how *you* felt, but you were a teenager, at high school, away from your parents.' He could almost hear the gears shift in her mind as she switched directions, focusing on the snippets of information he'd let slide. 'What was it you were hiding anyway?'

He wasn't going down that path now, it was water under the bridge and wouldn't help her with Jess, but he heard himself giving her more of an explanation than he'd ever given anyone. 'I didn't fit the private boys' school mould. I was hopeless at football, at anything requiring hand-eye co-ordination. Combined with a reputation for being a brain, not to mention being the tallest and gangliest in my year and coming from the opposite of a wealthy city-based family, I was a sitting duck for being singled out, bullied.' He stopped himself before he did exactly what he'd just said he never did—moan about his problems. Especially when the problems in question were in the past. They had no bearing on his life now.

He was aware of her gaze on him and wondered what was going through her mind at his revelations. She was probably regretting coming out with him for the day, listening to him carry on like this. He changed the subject back to what they were meant to be talking about. 'Do you think you've got to the bottom of it now? Does Jess understand? That's the key issue.'

'I think so but then an element of doubt creeps in. I'm wondering if I'll ever really know what's going on in Jess's life now. This is when I find being a single parent really tough. There's no one to talk things over with, work out the best approach.'

'Would you like me to talk to her? See if there's anything that she hasn't told you? Sometimes it's easier to talk to people we don't know as well.'

'I appreciate the offer but...'

'You're not sure.'

Steffi nodded.

'That's fine. The offer's there if you want to take it up.'

'Thanks.'

For once it was Steffi who seemed keen to shift the focus and she began to gather buckets and spades, shaking sand from their beach towels and collecting sandals and T-shirts. 'It's getting late, I think it's time to start packing up. Would you give the girls a five-minute warning, please?'

* * *

Despite their complaints about going home and their pro-testations that they weren't at all tired, the girls' eyes were closed before Steffi had even pulled out of the car park.

She was pretending to concentrate on driving so she could go over their conversation at the beach. Matt had offered his help with Jess. Because he thought she needed his help? Did he think she wasn't capable of managing on her own and was coming to the aid of a damsel in distress, or was he just being considerate? She didn't know. But he'd made it clear asking for help wasn't big on his to-do list, so she had to guess he didn't think too highly of her for all the strife she'd got herself into and had basically admitted she hadn't been able to handle. She'd pretty much told him she'd made a mess of things, financially, workwise, with parenting. All of it. And that was without admitting to the icing on the cake, the panic attacks. The least said about them, the better.

She pulled up in front of his house.

'Would you like to put Jess to bed in my room and stay for dinner?'

She hesitated, making a pretence of checking the two girls in the back seat. The fact that they were still sound asleep was the perfect excuse for him to make a quick exit but he wasn't doing that. Maybe she hadn't put him off for ever with her tales of woe. 'Can you cook?'

'Anyone can do scrambled eggs on toast.'

She laughed, tucking a strand of hair behind one ear, thinking that the day's end was looking brighter. 'As in-viting as that sounds, I really should get Jess home. We've got another busy day tomorrow. Mum and Dad are having their clearing sale this week and I really need to give them a hand with sorting stuff.' She could hardly say she didn't trust herself to be alone with him. One minute feeling down because she'd blown her chances, the next fantasising about an evening with him. She needed some down-time to sort her labile reactions out, that much was certain.

'Of course. If your dad needs any muscle tomorrow, give me a call.'

'Do you know some strong young men?'

He laughed. A rich, warm sound, lovely, just like him. 'I meant me. Tell your dad I work cheap. A couple of beers and a kiss from his daughter and I'll be happy.'

'The station hands will be around to do the heavy work, but thanks for the offer.'

'So no kiss either?'

'I think your luck might run to that.' Steffi undid her seat belt and leant towards him, closing the distance between them.

An image of him on the beach, gathering up their towels and flinging them into bags, jumped into her mind. He'd looked lean and brown, all sinewy muscle, at odds with his story of being bullied, but she could see in his build as a man the contours of the awkward adolescent he'd have been, before he'd grown into his frame, before those muscles had appeared. He must have been right when he'd said he'd not fitted in. There was something about him still, as an adult, that stood out, dragged her attention to him whether she tried to resist or not. His school peers wouldn't have seen the appeal he'd have as an adult male, but it would've been there. He had been born to draw female attention, without trying, probably without knowing. And there lay his appeal. And his danger.

She looked at his mouth, his lips parted in anticipation, and adolescent angst was forgotten, they'd talk of it another time. Her heart began to race as she moved nearer, tilting her head to one side. She could smell the tangy scent of the sea on his warm skin and could feel his breath on her cheek. She closed her eyes as she pressed soft lips to his face, tasting the salt on him. She held her lips still, against the corner of his mouth, half hoping that he would turn his head towards her but all the while conscious of the young girls in the back seat.

She heard him breathe out, felt him move his head, ever so slightly, bringing his mouth around to find hers. Gently he teased her lips apart with his tongue, exploring, tasting. But only briefly. As if he, too, was conscious that the time was not right.

He broke their kiss but left one hand on her thigh, the other resting against her cheek. His eyes held a promise of what was still to come for them, some time in the not too distant future.

'Thank you for a lovely day.'

'It was my pleasure.' He ran his thumb lightly over her cheek. 'I look forward to doing it again soon.' His grey eyes held her blue ones in an unwavering gaze. 'By ourselves next time.'

Steffi's heart somersaulted in her chest. There was no mistaking his intentions. They were the same as hers. She nodded as he climbed out of the car and opened the back door to lift Susie from her seat. Susie snuggled into his shoulder, fast asleep. She thought she'd never seen a more glorious sight. Matt adored his niece and Steffi had seen today that the feeling was mutual.

Matt whispered to her. 'I'll call you.'

Steffi nodded again and waited until he was at his front door before driving off, a smile playing over her lips as she drove away. She hadn't felt this excited about anything in a long time.

CHAPTER SIX

'OK, FOLKS, buckle up, we've got a short hop to William Creek, just five hundred kilometres away, and then on to Oodnadatta.' Ryan's cheery voice came through the intercom as Steffi fastened her seat belt ready for her second AAS clinic. Her second with Matt, too, as luck would have it.

'I'm sorry I haven't called you,' Matt said. 'I've picked up the phone several times and been interrupted. Now it's Thursday already and we don't have any firm arrangements.'

'It's OK. I know how quickly the time goes.'

'How's your week been?'

'Hectic, too. Mum and Dad held their clearing sale yesterday so at least that box is ticked and now they're frantically packing. They're due to leave as soon as Lauren and Jack get home from their honeymoon.'

'And you? Have you decided whether or not you'll stay?'

She nodded. 'With Mum and Dad leaving, I wasn't sure if moving back here would be the best thing, so I decided to leave things in the hands of fate to a degree. I went for an interview at Community Health on Tuesday and decided I'd stay if they offered me a job. I really can't do shiftwork any more. If I want to be around for Jess, I need regular hours and regular pay.'

'Have you heard from them yet? I'm happy to give you a reference.'

'Thanks, but I had enough referees. I got a call last night—I start work on Monday.'

'So you're staying?'

Was he pleased or not? He was hard to read. 'Looks that way.'

'What does Jess think?'

What do *you* think? she wanted to ask, but she said, 'She was more excited than me, but I think that might be because she thinks her chances of getting a pony have increased by about a hundred per cent.'

'You've promised her one?'

'No, but I think Auntie Lauren might have mentioned something.'

'Siblings. Can't live with them, can't live without them.'

'I always thought that quote was about the opposite sex.'

He laughed but didn't rise to the bait, choosing, once again, to change the subject. 'Put your sunglasses on and look out of your window. We're flying past Lake Eyre.'

Steffi took her sunglasses from her handbag, sliding them into place before peering out of the window. To their right was the enormous expanse of Lake Eyre, a huge, flat, saltpan, shining a blinding white in the sun.

'I can remember Dad bringing us out here once after a big rain, but I haven't seen it from the air before. There were birds of all kinds everywhere—pelicans, terns, sea-gulls. It was amazing to see all these seabirds so far from the sea.'

'How old were you?'

'I'm not sure, probably about the age that Jess is now. Why?'

'My parents brought my sister and I, too, but it was after the flood of '74. You wouldn't have been born yet.'

Ryan interrupted to announce that they were approaching William Creek. Steffi looked out the window again. 'There's nothing out here. Where's Ryan taking us?'

'Have you been to William Creek before?'

'Not that I recall.'

'I promise William Creek is down there. It's only got four buildings. If you blink, you'll miss it.'

'Where do we hold the clinic?'

'On the airstrip.'

'I beg your pardon?' Steffi could feel her eyebrows heading for her hairline.

'On the airstrip.'

'That's what I thought you said.'

'There are only ten permanent residents here and the only public building is the hotel. Most of our patients today will have driven here. We attach an annexe to the plane for shelter and set up under it. We've got everything we need on board.' He laughed and she assumed it was at the expression on her face. 'It's a good system, you'll see.'

Steffi couldn't determine whether or not Matt was pulling her leg. Even when they landed and she saw Matt and Ryan were erecting a temporary shelter, she still didn't really believe him. It took the sight of several dusty four-wheel-drive vehicles pulling up by the airstrip to convince her he'd been telling the truth. The first of their patients had arrived.

'Welcome to your examination room.' Matt waved his hand at the card table, two folding chairs and portable examination couch Ryan had placed under the tarpaulin. 'Can you take care of the children and babies, do their routine health checks and any immunisations that are due? You need to fill in their blue books.' He was referring to the book each child had in which immunisations and any childhood illnesses, as well as height, weight and other particulars, were recorded. 'And enter brief notes in this record book. The patient details will be transferred to their records back at the base. Sound OK?'

Sure, if being shell-shocked was OK. She was used to hospitals, for heaven's sake, big city hospitals. It had taken some adjusting to the smaller country hospitals and now she was working in the middle of a dusty airstrip in thirty-six-degree heat surrounded by buzzing flies. The retrieval from the station last week had at least had an element of excitement about it—but this location?

Her anxiety must have shown on her face because Matt reached out and grasped her hand. 'You'll be fine. I'll be right here. I'll just be in the plane, seeing anyone who needs a doctor. Just yell if you need me.'

He squeezed her hand and Steffi took a deep breath.

He'd be there. If he could be there all the time, maybe she'd never have another panic attack again. He'd certainly settled her down now without any trouble.

He winked at her and draped an arm around her shoulders, giving them a light squeeze before turning to go. 'You'll do great.' It was clear he was enjoying this, not enjoying her uncertainty but confident that she'd do fine, so enamoured of this environment that he could only feel excitement at the prospect of the day ahead. 'See you in a bit.'

'It'll be a once-in-a-lifetime experience.' She dropped her voice as she swatted at a couple of flies buzzing persistently around her face. 'At least, I hope it's only once in a lifetime.'

Matt laughed and turned back to the plane. 'Let's get to work.'

Steffi worked steadily for the next hour weighing, measuring and immunising a number of children and discuss-

ing everything from sleeping patterns to diet with their
mothers. There had only been a few patients she'd needed
to refer on to Matt.

Now she was sitting opposite Evelyn Mills, who was
holding a tiny baby dressed for the hot weather in a singlet
embroidered with roses, a nappy and a pink sunhat.
Evelyn had dark circles under her eyes but a proud smile.

'What can I do for you today?'

'Lynley needs her two-month immunisations.'

'She's gorgeous. Your first?'

'Yes.'

'How has she been doing?'

'Pretty well, if my friends' stories are anything to go
by. She feeds well, but often.'

Steffi looked at Lynley's chubby thighs and cheeks. 'I
can see that. You're doing a good job. Can I hold her?'
Evelyn passed Lynley over, and the baby looked up at
Steffi, content. 'Are you breastfeeding?' She was pleased
to hear an affirmative reply. 'What about you? How are
you feeling?'

'I'm fine. Just tired.'

'Believe me, it does get easier.'

'Do you have children?'

'One daughter. She's eight.' Steffi had found on several
occasions this morning, and at the clinic in Ceduna, that
the other mothers liked to hear that she was also a mother.
They seemed to like hearing about things that worked in
practice, rather than just in theory. 'Have you had your
six-week check?'

'No. Lynley's nine weeks old in a couple of days. Last
time the AAS was here she was only four and a half weeks
old.'

'Why don't I see if Matt can check you today? I can

do Lynley's health check and her immunisation once you're finished. Are you happy to see a male doctor?'

'I'm happy to see anybody, I'm just grateful that I don't have to drive all day to do it.'

'OK. Give me a minute, I'll see what he's doing.' Steffi passed the baby back to her mum and ducked around the plane, climbing inside. Matt was just finishing with a patient.

'Hi,' Steffi said as his patient left.

'Hi, yourself.' He was more rumpled now than when they'd arrived, and the sheen on his skin and his tousled hair brought images of roguish pirates flooding back. She suppressed a sigh. And her mental images. 'How's it going?'

'Interesting. Different. But I'm managing so far. Could you see a patient for me? Evelyn Mills, she needs her six-week postnatal check.'

'No problem.'

'Could you also see what she's doing about contraception?'

'Aye, aye, captain.'

She grinned. 'Sorry. I didn't mean to tell you how to do your job.'

'Don't worry about it. I'll need you to stay in the plane. It's policy to have a female nurse overseeing any gynae or obstetric examinations.'

'That must make things a bit awkward at times.'

'It can slow us down a bit, waiting until a nurse is free, but it's better to be safe than sorry.' Matt paused and she saw him study her carefully. 'Sure you're managing? You look worn out.'

She frowned at him. Exhausted she might be, but it didn't help to hear she looked as bad as she felt. Why did sweat, crumpled clothes and messy hair equate to gorgeous on him but looking exhausted for her?

Matt seemed to list mind-reading along with his numerous other talents. 'Don't get me wrong, you still look beautiful but I think you should close your eyes and get some sleep on the trip home.' The light in his eyes was full of good humour. 'I've got an ulterior motive. I'm hoping if you have a nap you'll be able to come to dinner with me.'

Steffi gave him a sideways glance.

'Nothing fancy,' he continued. 'A steak and salad at my place. Just the two of us. Could you manage that?'

'Your timing is impeccable. Jess is sleeping over at my parents' tonight so I've got a free evening. I'd love to have dinner with you, but,' she said, stepping away as he reached for her hand, 'if we're going to be back in time I'd better call your next patient.'

She felt like skipping down the steps. An evening together, alone. Alone with her roguish pirate. Perfect.

Steffi's eyelids were drooping before Ryan had even taxied to the end of the landing strip. It had been a long day. The morning clinic at William Creek had been followed by a longer session in Oodnadatta. At least there they'd been accommodated in the small hospital in slightly more comfortable surroundings. She leant back in her seat, letting her mind wander over the events of the day.

Was she was making the right decision to stay in Port Cadney? Things did seem to be working out better so far—she had a new job, Jess seemed happier, they had a roof over their heads and an attractive, intelligent man seemed keen to get to know her better.

She could feel him watching her as she relaxed in her seat. It was a comforting, safe feeling to know he was there. She was amazed at how in tune they seemed to be, how familiar they had become with each other in just a couple of weeks. They worked well together and each time she'd asked Matt to see one of her patients they had been in complete agreement about the course of treatment. Having worked closely with him on several occasions, she recognised his strength of character and his desire to protect and nurture. He was independent, a trait she identified with. He was reliable and calm under pressure and a good listener. But she still didn't know what had made him into the man he was today. He certainly knew far more of her history than she knew of his. It bothered her that he wasn't so open with his confidences, but maybe that would come.

Besides, she liked him.

She trusted him.

And for now, that was enough to go on.

She smiled as the now familiar rush of heat raced through her when she thought of Matt. She'd have some fun for a change. Pretend her life hadn't started heading down a short, steep hill to disaster, the crash hopefully now averted. Perhaps it was time she considered her own needs and desires as well as the demands placed upon her by motherhood and her career. They didn't have to make any promises, any commitments, just enjoy each other's company. She'd take a chance with Matt and see where it took her.

Steffi knocked on the door and a tingle ran through her when Matt opened it. He was wearing snug, faded denim jeans, frayed at the hems, almost white at the knees, and a brown thin-knit sweater, tanned skin visible in the V-neck, the sleeves pushed up to his elbows, leaving his forearms bare and Steffi at a loss where to look.

For want of a better option, she handed him the bottle of wine she held.

'Come in.' He held an arm out for her to enter then padded in bare feet down the hallway. She followed suit, kicking off her flat shoes when they entered the back room, and took a deep breath in, the smell of grilled meat and garlic pervading the air.

'Yum!'

'I thought you might be starving.' He looked a little sheepish. 'I am, so I've started cooking already.'

'Anything I can do to help?' She looked around at the table, already set with simple placemats and cutlery, a jug of water and glasses.

'You can open this.' He handed her the bottle of wine and a bottle opener. 'And pour.' He pushed two glasses across the counter to her.

'I'm not sure you struck me as the organised type.' She nodded at the table setting, the food already sizzling on the stove, plates at the ready. 'Impressive.'

'I probably don't take as long in the shower as you.' His clear grey eyes took in her appearance, and she was glad she'd taken the extra few minutes to choose her outfit, slim-fitting cream pants and a silky black top. 'And if I did, the results wouldn't be nearly as worthwhile.'

'Thanks. You can invite me over any time if you're going to give me compliments.'

He turned back to the steak sizzling on the grill, tossing sautéed mushrooms and aromatic garlic in a pan, draining icy water from asparagus and layering it on top of a salad of baby lettuce leaves and cucumber, placing slices of ripe avocado on top.

He knows how to keep himself busy when he wants to ignore a comment, she reflected as she watched him slip baked potatoes from the oven onto their plates. What was going on with him? He seemed to come near then back away again, let her know he found her attractive then close up on her again. Should she try again? Take the direct approach?

'You know, Matt, I haven't had a lot of practice with this boy-and-girl-make-friends stuff.' She picked up the bowl of salad and caught his eye. He gave a nod and she carried it to the table and waited there, watching as he slid the steaks onto their plates and piled the garlicky mushrooms on top, then brought their plates across.

He put the plates down and walked around to her, holding out her chair. He didn't break the silence until he was also sitting.

'Does that apply to us? Boy and girl make friends?'

'What else would we be?'

'I don't know, Steffi. It's been a long time since I've been involved with anyone, but it seems to me we're headed for something more than that.'

'You don't sound too happy about it.' Her eyes locked with his and she silently dared him to look away.

'I don't know what I have to offer.'

'What do you think you need to offer?' She vowed to get some answers out of him if it took all night.

'A willingness to be involved?'

'You're not?' Maybe it was best to find that out now. 'Are you?'

She leant her elbows on the table either side of her plate and put her chin in her hands. 'How long are we going to bat questions back and forth without giving any answers?'

A twinkle appeared in his eyes and he said, 'How long do you think?'

'Wretch!' She pretended to grit her teeth at him, knowing the tension that had been building had dissipated. But she hadn't gained anything. She'd have to work on her technique. She cut into her steak. It was perfectly cooked, juices flowing, mixing with the lusciousness of the field mushrooms. 'Mmm.'

'Good?'

She nodded, closing her eyes and savouring the flavours.

'Next time, I'll cook a proper Polish meal for you.'

Talk about mixed signals. Next time? But all she said was, 'Polish?'

'I come from a long line of cooks. My sister got the real foodie genes from my mum, but I can hold my own in the kitchen. Just.'

'Your mother is Polish?'

'Australian now but, yes, Polish by birth. My father, too.' The shutters came down again. 'Do you cook?'

Was a pattern emerging? Did he change the subject whenever anything personal, particularly about his family, was mentioned, or was it her imagination? He'd gone to boarding school but where was his home? She hadn't even known if his parents were alive or dead. She wasn't going to be sidetracked again.

She ignored his question, asking her own instead. 'How long have your parents lived in Australia?'

'Since before Anna and I were born.'

That was an answer. Of sorts. 'Where do they live now?'

'Up north.'

'Where's up north? Darwin? Alice Springs?'

'Outback South Australia. In the middle of nowhere really. Do we have to talk about my parents?'

'No. But what's the big secret?'

'There isn't one. I'm just not used to talking about my family. Like I said once before, I grew up not fitting in.

I'm not that comfortable making small talk about personal things.'

'Message received loud and clear.'

'It's not meant as a brush-off. But what can be gained by chatting about things like my parents?'

'Gee, I don't know. Maybe getting to know each other?'

'I can think of other ways to do that.'

One minute infuriating, the next too charming for words.

'Are you sure you're all Polish, you're not part-Irish?'

'Pardon?'

'Just making an observation about your wicked charms. What would you prefer to talk about, then, since your family tree is off limits?'

He shrugged, feigning insouciance.

'Us?' She suggested. 'OK. I'll go first.' Did a look of panic flash across his face? Too bad. He couldn't make all the rules. 'I think we need to work out where we're both coming from. At least, I do. If you're worried about us moving too fast, I want to go slow, too. My life is in a state of flux right now.'

She picked up her glass and pretended to be absorbed in the colour of the wine, all the while wondering whether now was the time to set the example of openness, tell him about her panic attacks, come clean. Maybe she'd inspire reciprocity and get him to spill a few of his own secrets. Then again, it didn't seem too likely, given what he'd just said, and his attitude on the beach about revealing too much, showing your failings. She decided against it. She'd already spilled most of her life story to him at Lauren and Jack's wedding. She'd edit her story, leave out some of the key details for now. There'd always be another time to confide in him, when they'd covered more ground, were more intimate.

She went on. 'But I'd like to see what happens. With you and me. And, then, of course, my focus is still Jess. That's one of the main reasons to move back, to give me more time with her.'

'Then we'll take it a day at a time.'

'I think so.'

'Good.'

And that was it. They ate in relative silence, chatting now and again about inconsequential things like the weather. Comfortable enough but it left Steffi free to continue the argument with herself about whether or not to push things with Matt. So he had issues with intimacy—or maybe just her. Should she let that dictate what would happen? Finally she decided she'd have to shrug off the female genes and not insist on digging up all the answers tonight for what was really only a fledgling relationship.

She put her knife and fork together. 'That was delicious. Thank you.'

'You're very welcome. Dessert on the couch?'

'You made dessert?'

'Sure.'

Steffi stared at him in awe—he'd done a lot in a short space of time—and he laughed. 'Actually, no, I'm not quite that organised. I just happened to have butterscotch-whirl ice cream in the fridge. And honey and double chocolate fudge and berry ripple.' He stood up from the table, pushing his chair back with his foot, muttering as he walked to the kitchen and rummaged about in the freezer. 'Or did Susie and I finish the chocolate last week?'

Steffi cleared the table while he started pulling cartons out. She stacked the dishes next to the dishwasher and Matt waved her away to sit on the couch.

'What's your fancy?'

'A bit of whatever you've got.' She tucked her legs up

under her, settling onto the comfortable, shabby couch, another contrast to the new extension.

'A woman after my own heart.' He came back to the couch and handed her an enormous bowl piled with huge scoops of multi-coloured ice cream.

'No wonder Susie loves you.' She put a spoonful of ice cream in her mouth and said, 'Look over there!'

'What?' Matt looked over his shoulder and Steffi leaned forward to steal a spoonful from his bowl, just quickly enough to slip it into her mouth before he realised what she was doing.

'Fank 'oo,' she mumbled, savouring the stolen mouthful. She swallowed. 'I couldn't resist. You had a luscious bit of butterscotch swirl in your bowl, all gooey and rich.'

Matt shielded his bowl in an exaggerated gesture of protection. 'The things we learn.'

They concentrated on their ice cream and when she'd finished hers, Steffi lay back in the couch, sated.

Matt took her hand and simply held it. 'You know this boy-girl-friends thing?'

She nodded. 'Mmm.'

They settled back, side by side, leaning into each other.

His voice dropped lower, found a husky note. 'Is it the done thing for the boy to tell the girl he thinks she's beautiful?'

'I think I read in the manual that's OK.'

He traced a finger along the contour of her cheekbone, sliding it down to her jaw, stroking the soft skin just below her ear. 'What does it say the girl does when the boy tells her that he wants very much to kiss her?'

She shook her head. 'I don't think—' her voice was barely a whisper '—there was anything about that.' The suspense was delicious.

'Shall we update the edition?'

'Yes. Please.'

With his fingers, he cupped one side of her face, tilting her mouth up to his, his thumb moving firmly across her cheek, caressing, proprietorial. His arm was about her waist and she snuggled closer, waiting for him to cover her lips with his own. And when it happened, the kiss drew them into their own world, their awareness focused solely on the here and now, the taste and scent, the feel of each other.

Steffi's hands fluttered to his stomach, feeling the lines of muscle beneath the soft fabric of his jumper. Lifting the fabric to feel the satin of his skin, she gasped as he pulled her closer, closing a hand over hers, moving it lower, exploring, inviting, before moving her hand back to her lap, stroking her fingers between his own, bringing them back to reality.

'No wonder the manual didn't have anything to say about that.'

'Maybe it was in the advanced edition.' She managed to sound flippant but inside her emotions were running riot.

'Where to from here?'

'You're the man. Don't you try and seduce me now?'

He laughed. 'You're not afraid to be upfront.'

'Does that bother you?'

'No, no, it doesn't. I like it that you don't play games. I like it that you're honest. But, I have to tell you, that still doesn't mean I know where this can go.'

She leant into him. 'It's OK, it's early days and neither of us knows that, but I *would* like to know what it is that makes you so reluctant to offer anything at all.'

'Will it help if I tell you it's been a long time since anyone has been this close to me? That I don't let a lot of people in at all? That's just the way I am.'

She stroked his jaw. 'Is that the best I can hope for out of you tonight?'

'Yes.'

'Then, yes, that helps.' And it did. Sort of. But although she thought physical intimacy wasn't an issue for him, it was hard to shrug off the nagging doubts. Why was he so closed emotionally?

'I enjoy spending time with you, I think you're beautiful.' He dropped a kiss on her mouth. 'Let's do what I suggested before and take this one day at a time. Get to know each other, wait and see.'

She nodded. She didn't see that she had much choice. If it was that or nothing, she'd take what she could get.

It was the mature decision, not diving in too quickly, not making rash promises that would have to be broken later. But she knew that if he took her in his arms again now, maturity be hanged. She'd throw caution to the wind and be his. All night. For however long he wanted, because for her one night wouldn't be enough.

Steffi slipped the blood-pressure cuff back into her bag and patted her elderly client on an arm that had seen too much sun over the years. 'You're doing nicely, Mrs Oatey, no hidden surprises today. Let's just see to your wound and we'll be about done.' She slipped a pillow onto the woman's lap and covered it with a sterile woven-fibre sheet, lifting her other arm and resting it on the pillow.

Mrs Oatey was a regular client of Community Health, needing weekly home visits for a variety of ailments, and, since she'd grazed her arm badly on an old piece of wood, daily checks.

Steffi removed the dressings, checking to make sure the healing skin hadn't caught on the cloth. Her paper-thin skin had quite literally torn away, leaving an angry-looking weeping wound. Steffi cleaned the area before applying the antibiotic ointment and rebandaging it.

'It's looking good. Karen will check on you tomorrow and I'll see you again next week.'

Heading off to her next client, Steffi reflected on the week so far. It felt like a week of new beginnings. Jess had started school yesterday and once she'd been introduced to her new teacher, she'd all but pushed Steffi out the door, happy in the company of Susie and her noisy little group of friends. And again today she'd gone off quite happily. A far cry from the Jess of last term who'd been dragging herself off to school.

On top of that, as much as she could tell after one and a half days on the job, her work at Community Health was looking good. The work wasn't stressful but looked like it would be varied enough to be interesting—and she'd get to know her regular clients, which would be a bonus. Her panic attacks seemed to be under control, or at least improving. Since she'd averted the one at Lauren and Jack's wedding, she'd been able to identify the beginnings of panic since then and talk herself through it. In fact, there had been hardly any instances of strong anxiety anyway.

She knew it was thanks to Nadine that she was on the path to improvement, but a certain rough-around-the-edges country man seemed to be a good-luck talisman, too. Hadn't things started looking up the very day she'd met him? She'd coped with the incredibly stressful situation of the tanker explosion with him by her side. And he was the one who'd been giving her kisses she'd never even imagined in her wildest dreams. And they seemed to have agreed to start *something*. She just wasn't quite sure what.

She cranked up the radio and drummed on the steering-wheel as she turned her car in the direction of her next visit. She had a date with Matt tonight and the mere thought of it was enough to send a little shudder of antic- ipation rippling through her. Finally, life was heading in a direction she'd never dared hope. Take it one day a time, Matt had asked her. She'd be a fool not to, there were just too many good things happening not to take the time to savour each moment. Her breath caught in her throat as she imagined tonight. Would Matt also want to take their relationship one step further? Maybe he'd see it as not taking it one step at a time, but she was ready. She could hardly think of anything *other* than Matt making love to her.

Her mobile rang and she pulled over to the side of the road to answer it.

'Steffi speaking.'

'Hi, Stef, it's Matt.'

The day seemed even brighter. 'How's it going?'

'Good. We're just leaving Kingoonya. Barring any de- lays, I'll be collecting you on time for the movie.'

'Just don't be early. I need time to make myself pre- sentable after work.'

'I promise you won't hear anything but compliments, Steffi Harrison.'

She laughed.

'I'm looking forward to tonight. What time do you fin- ish?'

'Three o'clock. I took a really quick lunch, I wanted to be able to pick Jess up from school. Are you sure Anna doesn't mind babysitting?'

'Of course not. And even if she did, she owes me some babysitting in return for all the times I've had Susie.' Steffi could hear humour in Matt's voice. She knew he loved having Susie around. 'So, how's it all going at work today?'

'So far, so good. It's a dream compared to my last job in Adelaide but I don't get to bump into any tall, dark and handsome men. Not under the age of sixty, anyway.'

'Glad to hear it. I'm the only tall, dark man you should be bumping into these days.'

Believe me, you're the only one I've *ever* bumped into. 'You forgot the handsome bit.'

Matt snorted.

'I'll just have to prove it to you tonight, until you beg for mercy and agree with me.'

'That could take a while.'

'I think you might be propositioning me.'

'You think right.'

'I'll pretend I didn't hear that.'

'Pretend away.' Steffi heard muffled sounds from the other end of the line before Matt spoke again. 'Ryan's heading for the plane so I'd better go. See you tonight—sixish?'

'See you then.'

Matt felt alive with anticipation as he turned into Steffi's driveway. He couldn't remember the last time the prospect of an evening out had held such attraction. The movie he'd chosen had received great reviews but a romantic comedy was not his normal taste in cinema. Then again, the movie was really irrelevant. Tonight was all about Steffi. The night was theirs and theirs alone.

Jess was sleeping over at Susie's, and Matt and Steffi could do whatever they pleased. Steffi wanted to take Jess to school in the morning but that still gave them fourteen hours. Fourteen hours to enjoy each other's company and start to make some new memories for them both.

Matt parked in the visitor's space and cut the engine. Grabbing his phone and wallet, he jumped out and slammed the door. Steffi was walking across the driveway towards him, faded jeans hugging her hips and a simple cotton T-shirt hugging her curves in all the right places. Matt paused by his car, concentrating on watching her and momentarily forgetting to walk.

Her fair hair swung about her shoulders and she pushed it behind one ear. Matt smiled and waited for an answering smile from Steffi, but it didn't come. His heart plummeted down into his boots.

'That's not a happy face.'

'I've been trying to call you.'

'I was on the phone. What's happened?' He held out his arms, waiting for her to come into his embrace, but she stopped a few paces short.

'Rick's just turned up.'

Matt's heart plummeted further. 'Jess's dad?'

Steffi nodded.

'From Saudi?'

She paced from foot to foot, avoiding his gaze. 'Somewhere there, I'm never quite sure exactly where he is.'

'Did you know—?'

'Ah!' Steffi ducked, covering her face with her hands, interrupting his question.

'What is it?'

'I thought it was a bee. I'm allergic.'

'It's just a fly.'

'Sorry. You were saying?'

'Did you know Rick was coming?'

'Of course not.' Her eyes met his this time. She looked like she was telling the truth. 'Rick's always been unpredictable. I've lost count of the number of times he's changed his plans at the last minute. It used to really bother Jess, so now I prefer it if he does appear out of the blue. It takes away any expectations.'

Matt tried to work out the effect this news had on their date. 'Why were you trying to ring me? Do you want him to mind Jess instead of Anna?'

She shook her head. 'I need to take a rain-check on the movie.'

'Why?'

'Jess sees him so infrequently that I like to be around for the first visit at least. A familiar face. Rick hasn't had much to do with eight-year-old girls so it's easier for everyone if I'm here, too.'

Matt felt his disappointment settle in the pit of his stomach like a stone. His perfect evening, their perfect evening, disintegrated before his eyes.

He couldn't help it. His automatic reaction was that Rick had made his choices years before, leaving his partner and their young baby, and yet here Steffi was, still trying to make things easy for him. Couldn't a grown man manage to care for his own daughter?

But, then, what had Steffi said? Jess didn't have much to do with her father and Steffi wished that could change. And perhaps Jess did need her mum there. Maybe he was being unfair. He could let it slide, he didn't have to make it into a big deal to reschedule.

'What about tomorrow night? I'm off to Coober Pedy tomorrow but I should be back by seven.' He waited for her answer, saw her avoid eye contact with him, and it would have been clear to the most amateur sleuth that she was hiding something from him.

'I'm sorry, tomorrow's no good either. The next night?'

'OK. I'll call you tomorrow.' He knew he was being abrupt but suddenly he didn't want to stand there, playing second fiddle to the mysterious, unreliable Rick. Rick who was no doubt probably rippling with all manner of muscles Matt would never have. He probably wore T-shirts ripped off at the sleeves and walked around with his arms tensed and pressed against his sides, all the better to delineate his bulk.

He waved a hand in farewell, mustered up a smile and headed for his car, his head full of thoughts he didn't want to be having.

What else had she said that night at the wedding? It would be better for her, too, if Rick were around. And that she found being a single parent tough at times—had she been waiting for Rick to reappear? Did she want him back in their lives? Was this her chance?

Matt turned the key in the ignition and the moment the engine came to life he reversed, spurred on by frustration, and took off down the street like a teenager behind the wheel of his first car.

The last place he wanted to go now was home to an empty house, and Anna's house held no appeal either. He was in no mood for her questions. He drove through Port Cadney, down the main street, past the hospital and found himself at the docks. Normally the feel of the sea spray across his face, the salty tang, the sound of the waves lapping at the hulls of the fishing boats was soothing, but tonight he had no desire to walk along the wharf. It would only remind him of Steffi and where they'd first met. He wound up his window to block out the smells and sounds and sat behind the wheel, gazing out across the water.

He was amazed at how disappointed he was. It was a bitter pill to swallow. He understood that Jess was a higher priority for Steffi but he hadn't seen Rick as a serious threat. And now here he was, appearing out of the blue, and immediately she'd put herself and Matt on ice.

He'd thought she craved security and stability for her

and Jess—she couldn't seriously think Rick was a candidate for that—but maybe he was wrong. What if she was drawn to unpredictability, to the bad boy, clinging to a female hope she could change the father of her daughter? Women did that, apparently. He'd certainly had his share of short-term relationships with women trying to get *him* to change, to be more open. But it had never had a chance of working, not until Steffi had come along. And maybe that was because he'd never felt pressured by her to change. He'd *wanted* to be closer to her, to let her in. Slowly, cautiously, but nonetheless to let her in.

He rested his head on the steering-wheel, forcing a halt to his train of thoughts. One cancelled date didn't mean that Steffi was about to disappear into the sunset with another man, even if the lone rider in question was Jess's irresponsible father.

Besides, the one thing he should be able to take for granted was that Steffi would never compromise where Jess's welfare was concerned. Stability was what Jess needed most. That, and her mother's time. And Steffi wouldn't achieve that by chasing pipe-dreams that Rick would change and give them what they needed. Even if she did still hold a torch for him.

He cringed at the corny language but they were the only phrases that came to mind, warning him that the bond he thought he shared with Steffi might be nothing compared to the ties that held her to Rick, even if she wasn't going to act on them. Wasn't there meant to be something magical, unique, life-changing about one's first love, teenage love? Especially if that had resulted in a child as lovely as Jess?

He thumped the heel of his hand against the steering-wheel in frustration. He wouldn't sit back and do nothing. There was nothing to be gained by that. When he returned from Coober Pedy he would lay his cards on the table. It didn't matter that he didn't know if he had much more to offer than Rick. At least he wasn't trying to play games. Steffi needed to know how he felt about her. It was time.

CHAPTER SEVEN

THE morning had sped by, Matt's energy fuelled by his decision to tell Steffi how he felt. He and Connor had completed the first half of the first-aid update and were enjoying a coffee with their colleagues, chatting and exchanging medical news.

With a population of a little over three thousand, Coober Pedy was big enough to need a GP, three nurses, a handful of nursing aides and some volunteer ambulance and fire officers who all had other jobs but were on call for emergencies. They were all here today with the exception of a skeleton staff of one nurse running the tiny hospital.

There was one thing a man didn't like, Matt reflected as he sipped his coffee, and that was a dilemma with no obvious solution. It didn't matter if the solution wasn't the right one, it was the being out of control that got a man every time.

Now that he'd decided on a course of action, he could put the issues aside and get on with the tasks at hand. He had a free night, the only positive outcome of Steffi's unavailability tonight, so he'd be staying over in Coober Pedy to catch up with the two locals most dear to his heart. His parents.

He hadn't told Steffi much about his mum and dad yet. But tomorrow when he saw her might be the right time to get everything out in the open. Before they got too deeply involved, he'd better sound her out, see if his background was an issue for her, like it had been for others in the past. That was, of course, if he could compete with Rick for her affections.

He was proud of his parents, loved them dearly, but he'd learnt in high school quickly enough how judgmental people could be. How quick to categorise others and how cruel. His parents were intelligent people who'd made some difficult decisions for the sake of their family, but because he was from working-class stock and his parents didn't speak English as their first language, he'd been treated by a lot of his peers as if he were socially inferior.

Logically, he knew it was stupid to let any of those early experiences influence how he acted today. Stupid to let an emotional response tied to the victimisation he'd experienced as a teenager have any impact on who and what he was. Crazy to let a time, when anything and everything different about him had been fodder for bullying, have an impact now. It hadn't mattered what it had been, once he'd been singled out, anything about him had been fair game. He knew that, knew it was all in the past, but emotional scars could be stubborn, and sometimes intellect was no match for feelings, for past experiences that had been painful.

He also knew he'd been carrying that burden over the years since but, then, experience had also kept teaching him he *didn't* fit in. Things had been fine at university, no more bullying, but he'd never been able to shake the feeling that he didn't belong. He had to admit, it might have been in his head, his thought patterns seared by his adolescent experiences, but even at university he'd known he hadn't quite made the cut. He hadn't been a true private school boy, hadn't had the connections, the wealth, the name. He hadn't had a single thing in common, in terms of upbringing, with any of his classmates. And yet he might have been embraced by his peers, they'd all become adults by then after all, but he'd probably distanced himself out of habit, out of a self-protective mechanism telling him he didn't belong.

And who, if faced with rejection for years in a row, wouldn't take themselves out of the game before it happened all over again?

On a logical angle, too, it couldn't be denied that he was different. He hadn't wanted to follow a traditional career path in medicine, hadn't wanted to run down the lines of specialising in a narrow field, treading the well-worn path to professional recognition and wealth. Even if he'd been brought up in the city with wealthy non-migrant parents, he just couldn't see that he'd ever have fitted the mould.

So from necessity he'd learnt to keep his private life private.

And then he'd met Steffi.

And known almost immediately she was different, more open-minded—the influence of being brought up in the country? Or had her circumstances made her less inclined to pass judgment on others? He thought so. Hoped so.

They had more in common than pure chemistry but he also knew that when Steffi met his parents for the first time he'd really be asking her to pass a test, to look beyond the man he was now and see the boy he'd been, the part of him that still wasn't sure if he could belong.

Enough thinking. He put his mug back on the table with a clink and cleared his throat, motioning the group to get back to the session.

Fate had other ideas.

The door swung open with a force that could only mean

'emergency' and Matt's heart sank for a split second as he realised his plans for today were about to go haywire.

The nurse on duty appeared in the room. 'There's been an accident, a mine collapse. About twenty minutes' drive north from here. A miner's trapped and apparently they can't get down to him.'

Matt grabbed his hat and medical kit, never far from his side, from the table and jerked his head at Connor and Bill, the local GP. 'Get the rest of the gear packed up and meet me out there with whatever resources you have.' He looked at Bill. 'Got your car here?'

He nodded in reply. They all accepted without question that Matt was in charge, even Bill. Matt had the most experience with emergency situations in unusual conditions. And he was a local boy, born and bred on the mines.

'I'll go ahead in your car.' He turned back to the nurse on duty. 'I take it the rescue team is onto it?'

'They've been called.'

'Whose claim is it?'

'Old Jimmy's.'

The adrenalin started to pump as Matt processed this information. 'Old Jimmy's?'

'You know him?'

There were lots of Jimmys out here. Most of the miners seemed to be called Jimmy, Steve or Johnny, but there was only one known as Old Jimmy who was on a claim twenty minutes north of town. His dad's oldest mate.

Bill's old four-wheel-drive was a vehicle after Matt's own heart, but it wasn't cars he was thinking about right now. The twenty-minute drive seemed interminable.

When he finally stepped out into the heat and the flies, the first person he saw was his dad walking towards him, arms outstretched in greeting.

'Mattias.' He used Matt's given name, and pulled his son close before holding him back and looking up into his eyes. 'What are you doing here?'

'I was in Coober Pedy, running a training programme. I was hoping to surprise you with a quick visit before we flew back.' He looked about the desolate location, red barren earth strewn with piles of old mullock, lumps of whitish clay Old Jimmy would have removed when digging the mineshaft by bucket and hand-shovel. 'But not under these circumstances. What can you tell me? How long's Old Jimmy been down there?'

His dad shrugged. 'I've been here for over an hour, so at least that long. It was just bloody lucky he asked me to come out here today or we wouldn't have known about this until who knows when.'

Matt shoved his hands in his pockets as he digested the situation. He knew the story all too well. These old-timers were paranoid about their claims and keeping secret what they were doing. Old Jimmy only ever worked alone.

Matt looked about him, taking in the scene. No one other than his dad and a few other old miners, together with himself and Bill, currently on the radio back to town, were here. 'Where is everyone?'

'The emergency response team is out at the open-cut mine on a training exercise and there's a carnival over in Port Newland so the young blokes have all headed there.'

'Damn.' In the absence of the response team, the younger miners would normally be champing at the bit to go down and rescue one of their own. Until they grew out of it, if ever, the blokes who carved their living from the earth would be on site as soon as word spread around, eager to flex their muscles and showcase their bravery. They'd be fighting over the chance to be first down the mine and add a few tales of their courage to their fund of well-embellished stories. But it wasn't to be, not today.

They walked to the entrance of the mine Old Jimmy was currently working, stepping around the lumps of mullock. The shaft was primitive, dug by hand with back-breaking tedium. A wooden ladder was bolted to the side of the narrow shaft, disappearing into its depths.

Old Jimmy was trapped down there, with no light source other than what he'd have taken down with him, probably just a head-lamp, and no means of communicating with anyone up here in the breathable air. Two-way radios, phones—nothing worked down in the mines. If he was even conscious and able to talk. Or even alive.

'What else do you know?'

'I came out here after lunch. Jimmy called yesterday, thought he was onto something big, said he'd know by this arvo and to drop by. I waited, he didn't come up, so I tried to get down to him and saw the collapse.' He patted his girth, nicely rounded after years of Matt's mother's good cooking. Lately, he hadn't been mining himself so he wasn't working it off like he once had. 'I couldn't get around the blockage, the passage is too small now. And to be honest, I didn't want to try. I moved some debris but the whole thing looked like it was going to cave in.'

Bill joined them, slipping his phone back onto his belt. 'The ERT are on the way but they'll be half an hour or more.'

'Hell!' Matt looked around him as though he might be able to see an alternative rescue team nearby. 'We might not have that long. We don't even really know how long he's been down there.' He stalked over to the car and pulled out his kit, returning to his father's side as he continued talking, shutting out thoughts about procedure and safety protocols that were fighting against his need to take action. 'I'm going down to have a look.'

'You can't. You have to wait for the emergency services.'

Matt snorted. 'I can't stand around and do nothing. A man's life may be at stake.' He was searching through his kit, choosing items and placing them in a strong plastic bag that could be slung around his shoulders, discarding others back into the medical kit. 'I've spent as much time in the mines as any of the blokes in the rescue team, probably more.'

His dad started to protest but Matt silenced him. 'I won't do anything rash, but you know as well as I do he might be dying down there. If I can't get him out, there'll be something I can do, even if it's to get access to put an IV line in. If he's injured, that might be enough to keep him going until we can get the equipment here to dig him out.'

'Then let's hope you're so darn skinny for a reason and you can make it through.' He handed over his helmet, fitted with a lamp. 'Just promise me you won't take any stupid risks or your mother will have my head.'

Matt kitted up and flicked the switch at the back of the helmet, turning on the light. He flung his makeshift bag across his shoulders and strode to the entrance to the mineshaft. It was years since he'd spent much time down in the shafts with his dad. The safety issues had never bothered him then, neither had claustrophobia, but as he turned at the entrance, ready to begin his descent, another surge of adrenalin hit him and Steffi's face flashed before his eyes. The reason he'd really wanted to see his parents today. Another reason not to go down. But he'd go crazy waiting around up top not doing anything.

Swinging himself around, he stepped down onto the first rung of the ladder. He worked his way down, feeling his way with his feet, getting a solid grip before moving his foot to the next rung, looking anywhere but back up to the surface where he knew his dad was watching him. Lower still—what was he, five metres down?—the walls of the narrow shaft changed colour again until finally the dark closed in around him and he looked down to see what was beneath him. The light was powerful but he couldn't see anything much down the narrow shaft. As he reached his foot down to feel for the next rung, he felt the support give way beneath him. For a spilt second he panicked until he realised the wooden ladder had come to an end and a rope ladder had been attached.

He kept moving, with more care now as the flexible rope was harder to negotiate. Past narrow openings picked into the walls here and there, wherever Old Jimmy would have decided he could 'smell' the opal and started to gouge with a small pick to work away at the dirt and rock.

Matt looked up and saw the small circle of natural light above him and at the same moment his feet struck against solid rock and he realised the vertical shaft had ended and now ran off in the narrowest of tunnels on the horizontal. Old Jimmy must have struck a seam of what he was convinced was a sure prospect for an opal-bearing pocket of rock and taken his digging in that direction.

He crawled into the tunnel, knowing it would widen slightly in the places Jimmy 'smelt' the opal. Where the tunnel was simply a means to take him further into the rock, it would be as narrow as possible. Labour-saving, yes, but making it a damn sight harder at times like this.

As he crawled into the tunnel, he saw the first evidence of the collapse. Only a couple of metres away, just where the tunnel widened a little, two beams had come loose from the basic ceiling props and had fallen across each other, one end of each still attached to the roof. They crossed over at the ground, forming a gate with only a narrow opening. He crawled up to it and squatted back on his heels and took stock. This must be where his dad had stopped. There was no way he could have squeezed through that gap. The question now was, could he?

He tipped his head back, the light from his head-lamp illuminating the top of the tunnel. The beams had come down but so far the rocky roof was holding. So far. It could come down at any minute, but if he was going to press on there was no point thinking about that.

He filled his lungs and blew out, psyching himself up for the next step in this journey. For the first time in all the years he'd spent down the mines, a sense of the walls closing in filled his head. Claustrophobia. 'Get a grip.' It was like a mantra. 'Keep moving.' It was a race against time. Not only for Old Jimmy. One false move and he'd be in the same position.

Reaching out, he placed a hand on the nearest beam in his way, gradually increasing the force he was exerting on it to test how secure it was. It held. Bending over, he eased one leg over the crossbar, trying to fold himself down as compactly as possible so his back didn't brush against the wall, his head and shoulders didn't hit the ceiling and his legs didn't put too much weight on the beam. Any of which could be disastrous.

He was over, but there was less than a foot's space before the next beam and he had to repeat the manoeuvres. 'Easy does it,' he muttered, but his heart was hammering and as he put his hand onto the beam to test its stability he saw he was shaking.

He crouched over the beam and had to twist to lift his leg clear, but as he did his shoulder hit the roof and a cloud of dust and rock fell on him. His heart in his mouth, he froze, waiting for the roof to come crashing down, obliterating him. When the shower of rocks stopped almost immediately, he made himself keep going. He was over. He squatted down, and wiped his face to get the dirt out of his eyes.

Less than two metres away, there had been a further collapse, much worse. Much of the roof had come loose, too, not just the props. The roof in between looked just as unstable. He asked himself why Old Jimmy had come down here—he must have known the ceiling had become unsafe—but he already knew the answer. If he'd thought he was onto some great gems, like he'd told Matt's dad, there was no way he'd have risked leaving the opals here until he'd fixed the supports. He crept forward and thoughts ran wild in his head. He even knew what would've happened when the situation had worsened today. He could almost hear the old miner muttering, 'Just a few more minutes,' as if some invisible force would hear and agree to hold the roof long enough for him to get out with the best find of his mining life.

He knew this because he'd grown up on the mines. And he knew this because, damn it, against all sense, exactly the same thoughts were flooding his head now, bargaining with the same deity to give him the time he needed.

'Eureka!' He whistled under his breath, afraid to disturb the surroundings.

Through a narrow aperture at the top of the pile of rocks and debris stacked up around the ceiling beams, he could see Old Jimmy.

He edged closer, shuffling his feet, balancing himself

with the tips of his fingers, his palms scratching the earth, and peered over the top of the nearest pile of debris. The man was immobile, slouched forward with his upper body pinned under a prop. He was in a tiny area—beyond him the tunnel was almost totally blocked—and his lower body was buried.

'Jimmy? Can you hear me? It's Mattias.'

No response.

Whether the older man had been knocked unconscious, had passed out with pain or had had a heart attack with the stress, Matt couldn't tell. It looked as though the falling beam and rocks had probably knocked him across the back of the head and neck before folding him forward onto his knees, trapping him there.

Matt eased himself forward. Could he squeeze over the top of the blockage? One wrong move and more of the roof could come down. He should leave, he knew that. He should wait for the response team to come with the right equipment to temporarily prop the ceiling and handle the evacuation. But from the look of Old Jimmy, they didn't have that sort of time. Protocol be hanged, he really didn't have a choice here.

Slowly, he began to pick rocks off the top of the blockage, stacking them to either side of his feet. He'd need to clear enough space before he could ease himself over the top. There was one beam still in the roof just beyond the pile. There was no way of testing whether that, too, was about to come down. He'd just have to hope like hell it would've collapsed with the rest of them if it were going to.

Rock by rock, like a game of pick-up-sticks, he continued to move the debris from the top of the pile. It seemed like hours had passed by the time he decided he'd cleared enough space to try. It was probably only fifteen minutes. And in that time Old Jimmy hadn't moved.

Matt closed his eyes. There was no room for fear or doubts, only for infinite care. Leaning his hands on the rock pile, he bent his body until his torso was almost lying flat on top of it. Almost in slow motion he lifted one leg clear over the mound, balancing as much weight as he could on that leg once it hit the ground, then following with the other.

He'd made it.

He crept towards Old Jimmy. Reaching out, he slipped his fingers to the side of the man's neck. No carotid pulse.

'Damn.' The word echoed.

He stretched a bit further, sliding his hand under Old Jimmy's chest, reaching for his arm. His fingers closed around his forearm and he wriggled them further down, searching for Old Jimmy's wrist. No pulse there either.

He was too late.

And there was no way he could risk pulling him free of the debris he was trapped in to attempt CPR. There was no point. There was nothing he could do.

'Sorry, old-timer, I was too damn late. And you were too damn stubborn.' Matt rubbed a hand across his eyes and squatted back on his heels just as the beam above creaked and shifted, the noise startling him in the silence so that he overbalanced and fell backwards, hard against the rock pile. He could feel the rocks teeter and then begin to fall around him, on him, one cracking him on the knee, hard, and then he looked up to see the ceiling beam move again. He tried to scramble to his knees and get himself back over the rock pile, away from the collapse that was about to happen, but his knee gave out on him, and he hadn't been expecting that. It caught him off guard and as the beam and rocky roof above him seemed to creak down closer, he knew he'd missed his chance.

He flung himself at the rock pile, desperate to scramble clear, but the collapse was quicker. His arms and torso were on the pile now but he hadn't been fast enough. The beam caught him square on the lower back, trapping him in a fall of rocks. He felt the force, an almighty blow, and still rocks kept falling, bouncing around him, hitting his arms and striking his head—thank goodness for the helmet—and it felt like a nightmare that would never end. He had to close his mouth and hold his nose shut, his eyes tightly shut, too, against the air thick with rock dust. He tensed his jaw, his arms, shielding his face, and tried to keep his panic in check, keep his mind focused on staying calm, not thinking, analysing, just getting through this alive, while the rocks built up around him.

It seemed an eternity before the collapse ended, and when he tried to open his eyes all he got was a face full of dust and it was some moments more before the dust had settled enough for him to keep his eyes open. The light was flickering and he thought, at first, that it was just the dust settling. Then he realised that it was his headlamp, presumably struck by one of the falling rocks.

He uttered a stream of abuse under his breath.

If he could pull himself free, then he could at least crawl down the tunnel and wait where it was less unstable and try to coax some extra time out of his light. He gripped the remains of the pile with his hands, tensing himself on his forearms, and then he tried to find a foothold with his feet, to give him an extra little bit of force to lever himself free.

'Hell.' If ever he'd had need for an expletive, it was now.

He couldn't feel his feet. His legs. Or his lower back. There was no way he could pull himself clear just with his arms when his lower body and legs were pinned. And especially not when his legs were effectively a dead-weight. The blow to his lower back must have done some damage after all, but he blocked out the implications. He couldn't think about that. He had to concentrate all his energy on getting out, on living through this.

He turned his face up to the roof, craning his neck in his attempt to see behind him. Was it safe to take his helmet off, so he could fiddle with the lamp and try to get it to hold out? He couldn't see well enough in the fading light. If he was going to have any chance of digging himself out, he had to take the risk.

There was another blockage just ahead, the one he'd first got himself over, and if he tried to continue in the dark, he'd be crawling straight into a booby trap. Although with his legs useless, there was almost no need to even think about getting free. It couldn't be done. But the thought of being trapped down here, imprisoned in what seemed more and more like a rocky tomb, in total darkness, was almost enough to have him lose his self-control totally. He had to try.

Gingerly, he slipped his helmet free and turned it over in one hand. He had just enough time to see that the wires leading from the battery to the lamp still seemed to be connected before the light flickered one last time and died. His heart sank with it as complete darkness closed in around him. He felt for the battery compartment. Maybe the batteries had been loosened by the falling rocks, interrupting their connections? He fiddled with the batteries, blindly trying to push them into place. Nothing. The mine remained pitch black.

He was aware of the noise first, and then the smell of dust around him. And then he felt it, the shower of rocks beginning again. He tried to close the battery compartment so he could put his helmet on, a voice in his head berating him for having removed it in the first place. There, closed. He lifted it to his head just as an excruciating pain shot up his hand, making him drop the helmet. He raised his arms over his head, but it wasn't enough. The next rock hit him square across the back of the head and, although everything around him was already dark, he knew that the darkness was beginning in his head now, too. If he survived this at all and they managed to pull him out alive, he knew he wouldn't be conscious to know about it.

CHAPTER EIGHT

'MUM, it's for you. It's Connor.'

Jess held the cordless phone out to Steffi as she dumped her bag on the kitchen table. She'd just got home after her appointment with the psychologist and had been thinking, not for the first time, that she'd have to tell Matt about her panic attacks at some point. Things had to be out in the open, especially if it meant she was avoiding dates with him because of it. Her appointment today would have meant a very late start to a date tonight. How did she explain everything that had been going on when she'd been trying to pretend all was fine?

She held out her hand for the phone, wondering why the paramedic was calling her.

'Connor, what's up?' She opened the fridge door, taking out a carton of orange juice.

'There's been a mining accident in Coober Pedy.'

A shiver of fear ran through her as she replaced the carton and closed the fridge. 'Matt was in Coober Pedy today.'

'I know. I also know you and Matt are close, so I thought you'd best hear it from me early on.'

The trickle of fear intensified and became like icy fingernails scraping down her spine. 'What's happened?'

'A miner was trapped and Matt went down after him. He was caught in a further collapse. They got him out, eventually. He's alive but he's being airlifted to Adelaide as we speak.' Connor paused and Steffi knew there was worse to come. 'He was trapped from his waist down. He

134

was unconscious but there's some concern about spinal injuries.'

'Do you know…?' She trailed off, unable to voice the fears creeping through her.

'I don't know what the prognosis is. I'm sorry, I'd only be guessing. We'll have to wait until the neurologists have seen him.'

'Where's he being taken?'

'Prince Edward's.'

'Where I used to work.' Thoughts raced through her head, bumping into each other. 'What was he doing down the mine in the first place? Isn't there a rescue team or something?'

'Yes, but they were already busy so Matt went down on his own.'

A cry escaped her throat. 'Why him? He doesn't know the first thing about mines!'

'Matt? Of course he does.' She could hear the puzzlement in Connor's voice. 'He grew up down the mines, his dad's a miner. But he still shouldn't have gone down unaccompanied, against all safety protocols.' Connor broke off and, in the background, she could hear talking. 'I have to run. I'll check in with you later. Are you alone with Jess? Do you want me to ring someone?'

'No, that's OK. Thanks for the call.'

'No problem. Let's hope we have some good news soon, hey?'

The line went dead and Steffi let her arm fall limply at her side.

Fear and anger were battling for recognition but she couldn't think straight, there was so much noise in her head, so many thoughts clamouring for supremacy. Matt was injured, maybe critically. He'd been trapped down a mine. He'd grown up down the mines. Why hadn't he ever told her that? What had possessed him to take such a stupid risk as to go down alone, without special equipment? There were no answers, and meanwhile Matt was being airlifted to Adelaide. This very moment, he would be secured to a stretcher and have an IV line in, a neck brace and goodness knows what else.

The thoughts whipped around, faster, faster, chased by unwelcome images of Matt, *her* Matt, immobile, unconscious, and suddenly she was gasping for breath. She was having a heart attack, she was going to suffocate—and all she wanted to do was run, run as fast and as far away as she could get from the nightmare. Everything about her seemed not to be itself, nothing was real. She staggered away from the kitchen bench, dragging in great breaths, but it wasn't enough, she couldn't get enough air.

'Mummy?'

Jess was in the doorway.

She had to get away and her body was poised for flight, edgy, heart racing, and she was looking wildly about the room for a way out of this madness.

'Mummy?' Jess was crying now. 'What's wrong? Mummy, are you sick?' A little hand held onto Steffi's arm but the voice was far away, hazy, unreal.

'Mummy? What's the matter? I'm scared.'

The thin line attached at one end to insanity and at the other to Jess, to normalcy, was running straight through her. She could feel it, tugging, pulling, cutting her in two, the whirl of panic spinning inside her.

'Mummy?' Little hands clutched at her and the feel of them caused the thin line to slacken, just a little but enough to tug her, unresisting, back to Jess, the simple touch seeping through the fog of unreality.

And she started to remember that she wasn't suffocating

or going crazy or dying. She was having a panic attack and the worst of it was over.

She was OK.

And whatever it took, she'd make sure she never had another one, never put her daughter through that terror again.

'Jess.' Her voice cracked and Jess flung herself into her arms, her head buried against Steffi's neck, her tears many and hot against her mother's skin.

'I'm sorry, sweetheart.' Steffi squeezed her tight, as if by holding her closer than close she could stop the last few minutes forming a memory for the precious daughter she'd just terrified. 'Mummy's OK. I'm sorry I frightened you, everything's OK.'

She kissed her daughter's hair, wanting to ease the fright away but she couldn't pretend it hadn't happened. Jess wasn't stupid, and it would only add to her confusion and fright. 'Matt's had an accident and he's being taken to Adelaide so the doctors can fix him up.' She dragged in a deep breath. 'I got a fright when I heard, a bit like you got a fright when you saw me so upset. But I'm OK now. I just forgot how to breathe for a minute.'

'Are you really OK?'

Steffi nodded and from somewhere dredged up a smile. 'Yes, promise.'

'Can we go and see Matt?'

'I think right now he's probably not allowed lots of visitors. I'll ring Anna and see, but Mummy might just go down to Adelaide to see him and you can stay here with Daddy.'

'Who's going to look after you?'

'I promise I'll be fine, sweetheart, and I'll ring you lots so you can hear for yourself. I'll only be gone for a couple of days. I have to organise our old house down there anyway, arrange to have our things brought here, now that we're staying.' She knew she was talking unnecessarily, but she had to prove to Jess, and herself, that she was OK, really OK. That she didn't need anyone to look after her. She'd always done just fine for the two of them on her own. She just hadn't known, until now, how much she'd started counting on Matt sharing that role with her.

Racing through the main entrance to Prince Edward's, Steffi didn't pause to look around the familiar surroundings but headed straight for the bank of lifts on the far side of the foyer. Pushing the 'up' button repeatedly she paced up and down while she waited for the doors to open. When it eventually did, she found she had it to herself and, after selecting the third floor, she sagged against the back wall, watching the numbers light up as the lift ascended.

She'd spent a sleepless night fretting about Matt, frustrated she hadn't been able to get on a flight until this morning. Anna had phoned from Adelaide. She'd got the last available seat, which Steffi knew was right but that hadn't lessened her frustration. She knew from Anna that Matt's condition was stable, although he'd sustained damage to his spinal cord but, as yet, they didn't know the extent of it. She had to see Matt for herself before she could take it all in. Hearing reports over the phone did nothing to calm her fears although she'd at least managed to avoid any more panic attacks.

The lift doors opened and she turned right towards the neurosurgical unit. She strode down the long corridor, forcing herself not to run, and crossed her fingers, hoping that she would know one of the duty nurses. Technically they didn't have to grant permission for her to visit Matt as she wasn't immediate family. She wondered if Anna had told him she was coming. Would he have asked to see her? He was probably too medicated to really know what was going on.

She breathed a sigh of relief to see Julian at the nurses' station.

'Steffi, how are you?' Julian came around the desk to hug her. 'You're here to see Dr Zeller. His sister told me you were coming.' She and Julian had been friends since they'd studied together, a friendship that had survived some tough times and one that hadn't diminished even as their lives had taken different directions.

'Julian.' Steffi kissed him on the cheek. 'How's he doing? Can I see him?'

'He's awake but the pain relief is making him drowsy. There's no one with him at the moment so you can pop in, but only briefly.'

'Five minutes?'

'Sure. He's in room two.'

Now that she was finally here, Steffi found herself reluctant to take the last few steps. She forced her feet to move forward until she was at Matt's door. There was a glass panel in it and through it she could see Matt. He looked thinner, lying in the bed, the white sheet pulled up to his waist, his chest bare. It was his height that gave him size and, lying down, his long, lean frame seemed to blend into the bed. But his face was the same, the perfect profile and strong cheekbones that she'd have recognised anywhere. She knocked a couple of times then pushed the door open.

Matt's head turned towards the door and his face lit up as their eyes met. All Steffi's doubts vanished and she flew to his side. He lifted his hand from the bed and she grasped it, bending down to press her lips to his, letting her concern flow out, hoping to heal his injuries through strength of will.

'Thank God you made it. How are you feeling?'

Matt's smile took half her worries away. Keeping hold of her hand, he said, 'The painkillers are taking the edge off everything. My lower back is aching and my head is pretty tender, but I'm actually glad to feel something. I wish I could feel my legs. I'd prefer them to be agonising rather than completely useless, like they are now.'

'What have the doctors told you?'

'That I was very lucky. I had an X-ray and a MRI scan last night, and I don't seem to have fractured any vertebrae, which was their first concern. I've sustained severe trauma to the spinal nerves, though, and they think that the paraplegia is from swelling and compression in the area.' He sounded OK about things, quite matter-of-fact. She knew she wouldn't have been so calm if the roles had been reversed. Was he really OK or was he still in shock or, worse, in denial?

'Do they think it's only temporary?'

'They hope so. They want me to rest for a few days and see what happens. They'll do further tests, depending on how things unfold over the next day or two.'

Relief that Matt had survived flooded through Steffi so that now fear turned to anger. 'How could you risk your life like that?'

'He was my father's best mate and like an uncle to me. I couldn't leave him on his own. I'm a doctor, I might have been able to make a difference.'

Steffi could see the pain in his eyes and felt contrite, thinking beyond Matt's physical health for the first time and realising that, of course, he'd see the miner's death as a failure on his part, even though there'd been nothing he could have done.

'I'm sorry, Matt, sorry for your loss and sorry for snapping. I wouldn't expect you to stand by and do nothing, but thinking of the danger you put yourself in frightened me.'

'It didn't turn out quite the way I imagined, I have to admit.'

She could see him becoming fatigued, trying to force his eyelids to remain open, smothering a yawn. She squeezed his hand and kissed him on the cheek. 'You need to rest. I'll pop back later today.'

Steffi took a taxi to her house, but even the familiar surroundings didn't lift her spirits and she wandered through what had been home, straightening pictures that weren't crooked, replumping the overstuffed couch cushions and wiping down the spotless benchtops. The plan had been to start sorting through her belongings, decide what she and Jess would need to take to Port Cadney and what could be stored or disposed of, but images of Matt kept floating in and out of her mind. Pictures of Matt as she'd seen him over the past few weeks. Vital, active. Playing in the sea with Jess and Susie, carrying Bobby from the burning fishing trawler, standing at the operating table in Theatre. Visions of Matt as the strong, healthy man he'd been—would be again, soon—bombarded her senses.

Her mobile phone rang as she was rearranging cushions for the third time in as many minutes.

'Stef, Rick. How's it going?'

'Better and worse than expected.'

'What's that supposed to mean?'

'It means that it seems he's escaped serious injury but there's a bit of a wait-and-see element to it all. He's not in the clear yet by any stretch. How's Jess?'

'Terrific. She had another good day at school and she's got a friend over to play at the moment.'

'You're coping OK?'

'No worries at all. Can't see what you women always complain about. Looking after a kid is a heck of a lot easier than working on oil rigs.'

Steffi bit back a quick retort. Rick was doing her a favour by minding Jess, even if she was his daughter, too, but Steffi would love to return to this conversation in a week's time. One day, particularly a school day, was not a good indication of the effort involved in raising a child.

'So you can manage for a couple more days?'

'A couple more? When are you planning on coming back? Don't you have a new job to get back to?'

'I only had two shifts this week while I get some clients handed over, and I've done those. I thought I might come back on Saturday, seeing as Jess is in school. Is that all right with you?'

'Right. OK, then, that should be fine.'

Steffi heard the note of panic and smiled to herself, but she wasn't about to let him off the hook. Rick was more than capable of looking after Jess, she never would have left Jess in his care if she'd doubted that. 'You can always call your parents or mine if you need a hand.'

'No worries, we'll manage.'

'Great. Tell Jess I'll give her a call after dinner. Thanks, Rick.'

Knowing that she had another day or two in Adelaide gave Steffi the motivation to get stuck into some jobs. She had decided to rent out the house initially and rent the unit in Port Cadney from Lauren. She needed to sort out her things and although she didn't have time to get it all done on this trip she could make a start. A few hours later their clothes and some of Jess's books and toys were sorted into three piles—one to keep, one to toss and one to give away. The clock on the wall showed it was nearly five so she took a quick shower, the timing right to get back to the hospital just after Matt's dinner.

'Hi, there. How's your afternoon been?' Steffi came into the room, like a much-needed breath of fresh air. She leant down, brushing a kiss on his lips.

'Dull. I can't stand lying around like this. I hate sitting still and I've never been good at doing nothing.' Matt cringed as he heard the whinging note creep into his voice, but nearly twenty-four hours of lying in a hospital bed was proving to be his limit. Thank God Steffi had been able to come to the city. Her visits were proving to be the highlight of his day.

'I've brought you some books. It seems to me like the perfect time to catch up on some reading. You've got a choice between two of the latest crime novels—one's a forensic crime book—and a couple of autobiographies. I noticed some similar ones on your bookshelves at home.'

'Thanks. The magazines I've got aren't holding my attention. Maybe I'll be able to lose myself in a good book.'

'What's been happening here? Anything interesting?'

'I've had physio, and a nap, and the nurses have promised me a sponge bath tomorrow. I'm not sure if I'm looking forward to that or not.'

'You'll feel a hundred times better after that, I promise you. Why are you apprehensive?'

'I haven't had anyone wash me since I was four, when Mum used to bath Anna and me.'

'You're not scared, are you? The nurses have seen it all before.' He saw Steffi trying not to laugh. 'Would you like me to do it instead?'

His complaints stopped. 'Maybe when I'm home again

and we can share a shower. Then I'll take you up on your offer.'

A faint run of colour swept across her cheeks but she didn't miss a beat. 'It's a deal. Have you had any other visitors?'

'Mum and Dad have been back in. I know this will sound ungrateful, but their visits are exhausting. Mum fusses around like a mother hen, chattering away nineteen to the dozen, and Dad sits in that chair over there and says nothing. I know Dad's feeling guilty over the turn of events and I'm sure that's the only reason he's making himself stay in town. He hates the city and doesn't like hospitals, too much evidence of weakness. He'd much prefer to be back in the country.'

Matt made a mental note to give his dad permission to return home, in a subtle way. Over Steffi's shoulder he could see the door opening and his parents appear. He realised with a feeling approaching dread that he hadn't thought about Steffi meeting his parents in this situation. It wasn't how he'd imagined it at all, but he'd have to make the best of things now.

Five minutes later he could feel the beginnings of a headache. He knew it was still the after-effects of the bump on his head but his mother's non-stop talking, her accent becoming thicker in her haste to ensure there were no awkward silences, wasn't helping. He'd never introduced them to a woman in his life before—that hadn't been his intention at this moment either—and it looked like his mother was intent on making sure this one couldn't get away. Even Steffi couldn't get a word in, but she didn't look too horrified. Still, he needed to stop his mother before she said something they'd all regret.

'Mum, do you think you could refill my iced water?

There should be a machine in the tearoom for the patients' families. The nurses will show you.'

Steffi jumped in. 'I'll show you if you like, Mrs Zeller. Then you'll know where it is next time. I'd better get going anyway. I think there's still a limit on the number of visitors you can have at a time.'

Damn. While he'd got peace and quiet again the goal had really been to separate his mum and Steffi. Now, not only were they still together but he couldn't hear what they were talking about.

Steffi walked beside Mrs Zeller towards the tearoom. 'You have a daughter? Jess?'

'That's right. I can't believe you know that.'

'I've heard a lot about you both.'

Steffi hid her surprise as she turned to put the jug under the ice machine. She'd heard almost nothing about Matt's parents and couldn't imagine Matt saying much about her. She was right.

'Susie has told me a lot about her new friend. Anna, too. You're a nurse, yes?'

Steffi straightened up, holding the jug of iced water in one hand, and nodded, looking at Matt's mum, searching for similarities between her and her son. They had the same facial bone structure with those amazing cheekbones and symmetrical features, but Matt obviously got his height from his father. She'd already known from the photo in his kitchen that Matt had inherited his father's incredible eyes. She'd given a silent 'thank you' to his dad at the time.

Matt's mother continued. 'I was a nurse, too. In Poland. But I couldn't work once we moved here.'

'Weren't your qualifications recognised?' She racked her brain, trying to recall what little she knew. They lived in Coober Pedy and his dad was a miner, but she'd only learned that from Connor after the accident. Talk about a closed book. The only piece of information he'd really shared had been that Matt and Anna had learned to cook from their mother. And they lived 'up north'.

Mrs Zeller nodded. 'That happened a lot. That was one of the hardest things about moving to Australia. I loved nursing. But I'm glad for the children's sake that we are here.'

'What did you do instead?'

'I took a job in the hospital kitchen as a cook. Apart from looking after my family, cooking is the other thing I love to do so I was lucky to be able to do that. Mattias and Anna used to come there after school while I did the dinners. They'd do their homework and talk to me. It was a good time.'

'You sound like you miss those days.'

'I miss having my children close by. I still know what's happening in Anna's life, she will pick up the phone, but Mattias…' She sighed. 'He keeps things close to his chest, just like his father. Since he went to boarding school all those years ago, I've never really known what he thinks. It's lucky he and Anna are close so I hear some things.' She paused. 'It seems he's quite fond of you.'

Steffi recognised the signs of a mother fishing for information. 'I'm very fond of him, too, but we haven't known each other long.'

'Sometimes it doesn't take long. Nic and I only knew each other three months before we were married. We've been married nearly forty years now.'

'I'm not sure that we're headed that way Mrs Zeller.' Oh, heavens, they had so many other things to sort out. What if she said something to Matt? What if he thought it was all coming from her, Steffi?

Mrs Zeller was still talking. 'Don't worry, dear, I'm not planning your wedding. But for Anna to have heard about you from Mattias, and met you, is quite unusual. You are obviously important to him.'

'It's very kind of you to say so.' Steffi's head was clear again, she could carry on a normal conversation. 'Matt's become a good friend to me. I'd better let you take his water back, I've got to get home.'

'Of course. I hope we see you again soon, Stephanie. I'm sure we will.'

Matt lay on his bed, watching impassively, as the physiotherapist put his lower limbs through their paces. He knew it was important to keep his joints and muscles mobile and, while he was unable to perform the exercises alone, physiotherapy was vital. But it didn't require his concentration, and his mind wandered to more pleasant topics.

What time would Steffi arrive this morning?

Would her hair be up so he could kiss her neck, or down so he could feel it swing against his face when she bent to kiss him?

Would she remember to bring some sultana grapes, as she'd promised?

'I know you doctors have a reputation for being awful patients, but do you think I could have a little bit of co-operation?' The physiotherapist's voice interrupted his thoughts, and by her tone Matt guessed that she'd been waiting for his attention for some time.

'I was miles away.' He grinned apologetically.

'Can't say I blame you. I want to turn you onto your tummy,' she said, as she put the bed rail up on one side. 'Can you use the rail to help me roll you over? You need to exercise the muscles that are still working.'

Matt grasped the railing with one hand and pulled himself over onto his left side, pushing onto his left elbow at the same time. He could feel one of Carla's hands on his hip and guessed her other hand would be under his knees. With her support and leverage, he managed to flip himself onto his stomach as Carla rearranged his legs.

'I'm just going to give your hamstrings a light massage, stop them from tightening up too much.'

'Sounds fantastic. Pity I won't feel it.' Matt rested his face in his hands and concentrated on his breathing.

His eyes flew open when he felt warm hands sliding over his lower back. He could feel the contact each time her hands reached waist level, but what her hands were doing below that he had no idea. But, more to the point, why were her hands on his back in the first place? When he had been at university the hamstring muscles had been at the back of the thighs, and he was pretty sure that's where'd they still be, accident notwithstanding. He cleared his throat as he wondered what he should say.

'Awake now? I thought that might get your attention.'

He craned his neck, trying to get it to turn 180 degrees, at the sound of her voice. 'Steffi?'

'Got it in one. You nodded off before Carla finished and she didn't have the heart to wake you. I offered to save her the trouble.'

'Thank God it's you. I was nervous for a minute there.'

'Thinking a pretty physio was about to have her wicked way with you?'

'When you put it like that, why don't you see if you can call her back for me?'

'Not a chance, Dr Zeller. You've got more than you can handle right here.'

He knew that for a fact. He couldn't handle anything in this state.

With Steffi's help he turned onto his back and tried to ignore the frustration stinging him. 'It's good to see you.' She looked so fresh and lovely, and he was feeling better just looking at her. 'How did things go with my mother last night?'

'Good. You never told me she was a nurse, too.'

'Didn't I?'

'No. You've hardly mentioned them at all.'

'Don't take it personally. I don't talk about them much.'

'Why not?'

'Why would you be interested?'

The man was more than a closed book, he was a slammed-shut tome wedged between heavy bookends. 'For starters, they've had fascinating lives and made lots of sacrifices for you and Anna. I'd have thought you'd be proud of them.'

'I am, but that doesn't have to translate into telling all and sundry my life story.' It came back to him that before he'd gone down the mine he'd decided to tell her more about his background. He'd forgotten that until now. But he'd have postponed it in any event. Lying in a hospital bed wasn't the right place. Besides, she'd met them for herself now—what more was there to say at this point? 'You'd be surprised how many people don't think so kindly towards people like them.'

'Maybe, but I'm not those people.' She'd let him think about that, think about whether he'd been right to shut her out quite so fully. 'Besides, I can see lots of similarities between your mum and me. We both want what's best for our children and we're both nurses—'

'Mum's a cook now.'

'And I love to eat.' She suppressed a sigh. He was determined to keep his own counsel on his family history and she wouldn't convince him to trust her by forcing the issue.

He shrugged, the gesture noncommittal.

'She misses you.'

'What do you mean?'

'She says you don't call her often enough.'

'I could speak to her six times a day and she'd still want to hear more. I love her but I can't make up things to talk to her about.' It didn't sound as if his mother had frightened Steffi away. Instead, it was starting to sound as though she now had Steffi convinced to get on his case about being more open in his life. Understandable, maybe, if they were going to get involved with each other, but uncomfortable nonetheless. Lucky, then, that he'd mastered the art of swift subject changes. 'You haven't told me how long you're planning on staying in Adelaide.'

'I've got to go back tomorrow, I want to be back for the weekend with Jess. I thought of flying her down here so we could make a start on sorting out the house in between visiting you, but I'm not in the right frame of mind to tackle that at the moment.'

'You can't stay for the weekend? Your parents wouldn't mind having Jess for a couple more days.'

'Jess isn't with Mum and Dad.'

He frowned. 'Where is she?'

'Her dad's looking after her.'

Matt's eyes widened slightly as memories flashed past and more things that had been knocked out of him by the blow to his head started to trickle in. Especially Steffi cancelling their movie date because Jess's dad had turned up out of the blue. What they'd been going to see he couldn't recall, but the overwhelming feeling of disappointment came surging back just thinking about that night. And he'd planned to have a heart-to-heart with her but he'd had the accident instead. Obviously they'd never had that discussion so where did that leave things between them? And where did it leave things with Steffi and Rick? What had happened during those hours he'd now lost?

'Matt?'

'Hmm?'

'What's wrong? You've gone awfully pale.'

'Headache.'

'Shall I call for the nurse?'

'No. I think I just need to rest.'

'I'll come back later. Oh, the grapes are in a bowl here.' Steffi pointed at the bedside cabinet. 'They're sweet and juicy. Enjoy.' She bent to kiss him, a gentle kiss that barely brushed the corner of his mouth but still it sent waves of longing through his body and started the flood of questions off again. Did they have a future? Would he be able to compete with the father of her child? What if he was left permanently disabled? Would she want him then?

Matt closed his eyes before the door had clicked shut, blocking out the vision of Steffi walking out of his room. An hour ago he had imagined feeding those grapes to her, but now he just wanted to pick up the bowl and hurl it across the room in frustration.

The accident didn't change the fact that he still had things to say to her, but he'd be blowed if he'd say them while he was lying flat on his back in a hospital bed.

It was Saturday morning before Steffi got back to the hospital, dropping in on her way to the airport. Pushing open Matt's door, she was surprised to see Anna in the room but not Matt.

'Steffi! Hi. I just tried to call you.'

'Why? What's the matter?'

'Matt's gone down for a myelogram, the specialist just organised it. Matt wasn't sure what time your flight was and wanted me to tell you not to bother coming past here first.'

'Why does the specialist want to run that test now? What's happened?'

'Nothing's changed, but I gather that's the problem. The neurologist seems to have expected some improvement by now. I can't say I quite understand what a myelogram is, though.'

'It's a test they use to examine the spinal nerves more closely. They'll inject a water-soluble dye into the fluid that surrounds his spinal cord, and then take X-rays. The dye will flow out along the nerves and on the X-rays it will show if the pathways are being compromised. I know the specialists were thinking that Matt's paralysis was from swelling around the spinal cord, but it sounds like they're checking for more serious damage.'

'Like what?'

'Nerve damage that may be permanent.' Her heart sank. She'd known this might happen but had been holding out hope that everything would be OK.

'Oh, poor Matt.'

Anna's words echoed Steffi's thoughts but she tried to remain positive. 'It might not be the case. We'll have to wait and see. But the myelogram is a pretty unpleasant test and they don't do it unless there's a real need.' Steffi glanced at her watch. It was already ten o'clock. 'Did anyone say what time he'll be back?'

'No. They only came for him about fifteen minutes ago.'

'He won't be back before I need to leave. Will you give him my love and tell him I'll call when I get home?'

'Of course.' Anna hugged Steffi. 'Take care and have a good flight.'

'Thanks.'

Her flight was uneventful, even arriving in Port Cadney on schedule. Arriving home to an empty unit, her first thought was to place a call to Matt. Her thoughts had been with him almost exclusively since she'd left Adelaide. Dialling the hospital and Matt's direct room extension, she was surprised when it was answered by one of the nurses, one she didn't recognise.

'Prince Edward Neurosurgery. Can I help you?'

Steffi realised the call had been diverted to the nurses' station and was momentarily thrown. 'Oh, uh, hi. This is Steffi Harrison. I'd like to speak to Matt Zeller in room two.'

'I'm sorry, he's diverted his phone. He must be resting.'

Steffi could tell the nurse wasn't about to offer to go and check. Why couldn't Julian have been on? Should she push her? No, she might be busy and Steffi didn't want to be the type who hassled the nursing staff. She'd been on the receiving end of that more than she liked herself. She knew, too, that she'd get no other information as she wasn't family.

'Could you let him know I called, please?'

'Sally, was it?'

She bit back a sigh. 'Steffi.'

'Right.'

Replacing the phone, she stared at the wall. Was he OK? Her stomach had just been invaded by a swarm of agitated flying insects, definitely too unsettled to be described as butterflies. More like marauding locusts. Was he really just resting or had he had bad news?

CHAPTER NINE

'It's good to have you back. You, too, brother-in-law,' Steffi said, her greetings mixing with those of the newly-weds as she hugged first one, then the other, before they carried the bags inside Lauren's flat, still talking. 'How was it?'

'Wonderful,' they replied in unison, Jack looking adoringly at his new wife. Lauren threw her bag down on the floor and Jack rolled his eyes at Steffi as they both reached out to pick it up and put the pile of luggage in the main bedroom. 'I'll let you two natter for a few minutes and start sorting through this lot.' He gestured to the bags at their feet. 'Give me a call when the kettle's boiled. I imagine that's where your sister's disappeared to.'

'One white tea, no sugar, coming up.'

Lauren was already in the kitchen, opening windows and flicking through the mail Steffi had collected for them. 'Anything to report on back at the ranch?'

'Literally or figuratively?'

'Both. Nothing new on the station? With you?'

Steffi took the easiest question first. 'All under control with the property but, then, Dad's the one to ask about that. They're champing at the bit to make the move now, even Dad.'

'And we can't wait to make the move to the farm.' She filled the kettle and flicked it on before perching on a kitchen stool. 'What about you? Looking forward to getting settled in here properly with all your things around you?'

Steffi shrugged.

'What's the problem? You were so keen on the new plan. Changed your mind already?'

'No. Things have just got a little weird since you've been gone. No.' She shook her head, correcting herself. 'Not weird, just…complicated. Matt and I seemed to be getting somewhere…' She filled Lauren in on the scant details she'd felt sure of a week or so ago. 'Then Rick turned up and Matt had an accident, injured his back, and has been in the Prince Edward ever since.'

Lauren had just stood up from her stool but, on hearing the news, sat back down. 'Is he OK?'

Steffi shrugged again, leaning back against the kitchen counter. 'The specialists say he'll be flown home tomorrow, because there's nothing else that can be done for him at this stage. The diagnosis is temporary paraplegia due to soft tissue damage and swelling around the spinal cord but the tests were all inconclusive.'

Lauren nodded. 'But, in theory, things should resolve in time.'

'From what Anna tells me, he should be making progress even now, but he's not, and the doctors aren't sure why he's not improving.'

'From what Anna tells you? What about Matt?'

'He's not taking my calls.' Steffi slumped against the bench. 'At least, that's all I can assume, given that I've rung every day over the weekend and I never get to talk to him. There's one excuse after another. He's gone for another test, he's resting, he's asleep, his phone's been diverted.'

'Couldn't that be the case?'

'Twice a day, no matter what time I ring?'

'But why the sudden change?'

A third shrug. 'I don't know. Either he's changed his

mind about us, or he's still annoyed that I cancelled a date with him when Rick turned up, although he was happy enough to see me in the hospital. But the day I came back to Port Cadney he wasn't in his room when I went to say goodbye. Anna says she told him I'd been and that I've called, but I haven't heard anything at all from him.'

'He's probably got a lot on his mind.'

'I know that. I'm not trying to pressure him but a brief conversation would be nice, some emotional connection. But he's just shutting me out. I don't know what happened.'

'Guess you'll find out tomorrow.' Lauren stood up, taking three mugs from the cupboard. 'By the way, what's happening with your panic attacks?'

'I had one when I heard about Matt's accident and Jess saw it. I terrified the poor baby. I've seen Nadine twice since then and she seems to agree that I've finally turned a corner, mostly because I'm adamant that I'm never going to put Jess through that hell again.'

'And Rick? Where does he fit into all this?'

'Whoever knows *where* Rick fits in.' Steffi turned away. 'Isn't that kettle boiling yet?' She walked across the kitchen to check on it. 'It helps if you turn it on at the wall switch, Lauren.' She turned back to catch the smirk on her sister's face. 'You did that on purpose so you could quiz me.' Lauren laughed and Steffi waved a teaspoon at her. 'Bad, little sister, very, very bad.'

Yes, it was bad, very, *very* bad, reflected Steffi as she sat in Matt's sunny lounge room the next afternoon, looking at Mrs Zeller over a glass of water. She shifted uncomfortably in her seat, her uniform feeling tight and hot after a day's work. Although none of that was actually what was bad.

Matt was asleep.

Or so Mrs Zeller was saying. But the way she couldn't quite meet Steffi's eyes was telling a different story, and the fact that she'd heard Matt's voice coming from the master bedroom at the front of the house as she'd knocked only added weight to her suspicions.

So where did that leave her? Apart from feeling unwanted and very, very silly.

Steffi tapped her feet as she perched on the couch where only weeks before she'd sat with Matt, flirting over ice cream. What a lot of changes there had been since then. None of them good, except for Jess having Rick back in her life—but even that had a dark side. She was pretty sure Rick's arrival had something to do with Matt's change in attitude towards her.

'Another drink, dear?' Matt's mother asked in her accented English. Her eyes were kind, reflected Steffi, and the nervous over-talkativeness she'd seen on their first meeting seemed much more under wraps today.

Steffi shook her head. 'No, thanks, Mrs Zeller, I don't want to keep you. I just thought Matt might be up for a visitor...' Her words trailed off and she felt embarrassed all over again because they both knew Matt just didn't want *her* as his visitor.

'He's not doing too well, dear. Don't take it to heart, he's just having a difficult time with his injury. I'm not sure whether having me as his home nurse will make things better or worse. It might make him focus less on being a patient, but there is the risk I'll drive him mad.' She smiled but the stress lines around her mouth and eyes didn't soften.

'You're home-nursing him?'

The older lady nodded. 'It seemed the best option. I wanted to stay down here and this way there was one less body in the house and one less bag of medical bills.' She stopped talking and fixed Steffi with a penetrating look. 'I'm sure Mattias will want to see you soon. Please, don't give up on him.'

Don't give up on him. What was that supposed to mean? Her bewilderment must have shown in her face.

'Sometimes it's best to let things sit as they are for a time, see what happens,' the older woman said.

Wasn't that at odds with not giving up on him? One more piece to a puzzle that was really flooring her. The thought of puzzles jogged her memory.

'Jess would like to see him. Matt had promised to help her with her latest jigsaw puzzle. Can you check if that's OK with him at some stage, when he's feeling a little better? If it's easier, I can drop her off for an hour and then pick her up, if that's not too much trouble for you. She'd just really like to see him, and she's been very upset about his accident.' Good grief, now she'd caught the nervous-over-talking bug. She snapped her mouth shut.

'I'm sure in a few days or so that will be just what the doctor would order.'

Whereas it's pretty clear I'm exactly what the doctor's taken *off* the menu. The bitterness in her tone as the words rang out in her head surprised her. Matt not wanting to see her now didn't mean for ever. Not necessarily. And in the meantime, she had a lot of things to sort out with Rick.

One problem after another. Was that all life was?

She suppressed a sigh, not wanting to sound like a worn-down old woman, and stood up, stretching her hand out to Mrs Zeller. 'Thank you for the water, and the chat. It was nice to get to know you a little better, just a pity it wasn't under happier circumstances.'

Mrs Zeller took her hand and stood up, too. 'They'll come again, dear, they always do.'

They walked to the front door.

'Give my...' Steffi paused. What should she say—regards, love, best wishes? She bit the bullet, going for broke. 'Give my love to Matt, and wish him all the best. I'll be in touch with you, to see about Jess coming for a quick visit.'

'Thank you, Stephanie.' Her name sounded unusual with Mrs Zeller's pronunciation, and she liked it. Not that she'd have much reason to hear it in the future if Matt kept avoiding her.

Matt heard their voices grow louder as they neared the front door. Heard Steffi send him her love, wish him all the best. Heard the front door close and knew his mum would come immediately into his room in the hope of finding out why he'd refused to see her. So he did what any self-respecting male wanting to avoid a grilling would do and closed his eyes and pretended to be asleep. He'd have rolled over, too, but, of course, that wasn't an option for him.

He heard the door creak and could imagine his mum peering around it, judging whether to leave him or come in. The door closed and he heard her padding back down the hall, no doubt to make him some more of her amazing dumplings for lunch. Maybe it was a good thing he had scarcely any appetite or he'd be the size of a house if she kept trying to feed him like that, while he was lying uselessly in bed, half a man, no good to anybody.

Steffi's car spluttered to life in the driveway. It sounded much like his, unpretentious, probably unreliable, and no doubt the only one she could afford, just as his had been when he'd bought it. He'd been unkind not to see her, but that thought passed quickly enough when he tried to change position in bed and remembered again that he couldn't.

He'd not had the slightest twinge of feeling below his lower back since he'd woken in a hospital bed in Adelaide. The only thing that had been returning was exactly what he *didn't* want. Memories of the accident. Old Jimmy's lower body crushed beneath the rocks and beams. *Just like mine*, the negative little voice that was ever-present now in his head told him. The collapse trapping his legs. The light on his helmet going out. The feelings he'd fought against, the terror and helplessness that had come from being trapped, imprisoned in a dark tomb. Slowly, more and more images were being added to the stockpile of memories he didn't want to have.

He knew this was normal. To think about the event, re-experience it, even. It was normal to be stressed by what had happened. It was, after all, less than a week since the accident and only a day since he'd been flown home from hospital.

But was it normal to feel like he'd never walk again? For the doctors, the nurses, the physiotherapists all to cajole him along when it was bloody obvious it was all over for him?

He was a cripple.

Useless.

And most definitely useless to Steffi. He wasn't even sure she'd wanted him when he'd been whole, when his limbs had functioned. She'd pushed him away the moment Rick had reappeared. He shut out thoughts that she'd come to him in the hospital—hadn't she needed to come to Adelaide anyway, to tie up loose ends?—and that she'd been calling him, had come to see him here.

He opened his eyes again and looked down the length

of his bed, seeing the way his immobile legs made little hillocks under the thin blanket. Where was he meant to go from here?

Steffi's weekend was spent moving things between the farm and Lauren's unit, with lots of negotiation along the way about what furniture to leave and take, what their parents would take with them the next week when they made the shift to the city, how to agree between Jack's kettle and Lauren's.

'You won't turn a kettle on, anyway, Lauren, from what I've seen, so you might as well give both to me.'

'The kitchen table should stay as it is, dear, to make sure there's lots of room for the big family reunions that *you'll* be cooking for now.'

'Then you should keep my table, Stef.'

'Anyone want an old wardrobe? Complete with moth-ball coat-hangers?'

And so it went on. Good-natured banter, deciding between a lifetime of memories on the farm, delegating, offering, no fights, no bickering over furniture. Just as it should be, thought Steffi. By the end of the weekend, she had more furniture to her name then she'd ever had. But she'd have traded it in an instant for the chance to talk to Matt.

Rick even pitched in to help, mainly by looking after Jess, but that was more than he usually did. And it was showing. There was a new brilliance in Jess's eyes, a new spring in her step. She was coming along in leaps and bounds, things were working out for her.

By Sunday evening, Steffi was ready to collapse in Lauren's unit—*her* unit now—but Rick would be dropping Jess off any minute so she didn't have that luxury.

She contemplated having a shower but the doorbell

ringing to herald their arrival eradicated that possibility and, tired as she was, she was certainly looking forward to seeing her little girl. She felt she'd hardly seen anything of her lately.

'Hello, sweetheart.' Jess flew into her arms the moment the door was opened, and Rick loped inside behind her, dropping a kiss on Steffi's cheek.

'She's had her dinner and a bath. She's pretty well pooped out so…' he motioned behind him to a box on the ground filled with take-away containers '…I thought we might get her off to bed and have a talk.'

It was the last thing Steffi felt like. The very last. But it was also the first time he'd taken any initiative when it came to talking—it would be about Jess, of course—so she said yes. And when their daughter was tucked up in bed and she came out to find Rick had served the food and even set the table, it was all she could do to stop her jaw from hitting the floor.

When they were both seated and served, Rick said, 'It's nice here, Steffi, being back in the old town. Good for Jess, I think.'

'Yes,' she said with some difficulty around a mouthful of rice, tofu and prawns. She swallowed. She may as well articulate what had been playing on her mind the last few days. 'It *is* nice. Would you ever consider moving back here? To be close to Jess, be a hands-on dad?' She could see from his startled expression he hadn't been expecting that. She'd long ago given up on asking him for anything, let alone to move his life. 'Being back in Port Cadney is exactly what Jess needed, but she's even happier now you're back. She needs a dad, she needs a male role model. A constant in her life.' From the look of things, that role wasn't going to go to Matt. And, by the way

Rick was shifting in his chair, he didn't want the gig either.

Rick laid his chopsticks down across his bowl. Not a good sign, because not much came between Rick and his food. 'When I said we should talk, that wasn't what I had in mind.'

'I know I've dropped this on you...' Although she couldn't help thinking, You *have* had *eight years* to think about it, really. 'But you've been great with her this week. You've changed, or maybe it's because she's older now, I'm not sure.' She was rambling again, but she felt a sudden urgency to convince him, to go in to bat for Jess and what she needed.

'Maybe a bit of both.'

'So can't you at least think about it? For Jess?'

'I could say I'll agree to that, Steffi, but it wouldn't the case. My life isn't here.'

Steffi interrupted him. 'Your daughter is.'

He ignored her. 'My work isn't here.'

She interrupted again. Who cared if it wouldn't get them anywhere? 'What work, Rick? You've never stuck to anything longer than a month.'

He grinned at her. Typical Rick. Impossible to offend. Laid-back. Easygoing. Far, far too much so to ever be an effective parent, to ever share the responsibilities with her. 'That's different now.'

'Is it? Is it really?' She felt like his mother in this relationship, a relationship based on the fact they'd created a beautiful human being together. But there, it seemed, his adult responsibilities had ended for ever.

'Yes, doubting Steffi, it is. I've got a long-term contract with an oil company in Saudi Arabia. It's great money, and I'm happy doing it. And that's one of the reasons I wanted to come here now rather than wait for the next school holidays. I've got something to give you.' He pulled out an envelope from his back pocket and handed it to her, creased and crushed from him sitting on it for goodness knew how many hours.

'Open it.'

She did and saw a bulging wad of notes.

'My first month's wages.'

Steffi opened her mouth to protest but he silenced her. 'It's the very least I owe you. And from now on I'll send money regularly, if you'll give me the details. I *want* to help. I feel bad I've only given you the odd bit here and there over the years. It's just that you never asked and you always seemed to be doing so well. I guess it was easy to tell myself you didn't need anything from me.'

'I *did* ask you, Rick. But there was always an excuse, no matter what the request was.' She shook her head. 'Look, it really doesn't matter any more, so let's not go on about it. One thing I *do* think you owe Jess, though, is to let us know what role you're going to play in her life. Can we make some plans about when you're going to see her and, if we do that, can you stick to them? She has a right to see you and to know when you're coming, so she can look forward to it and I can help her be excited about it. You owe her that. And me.'

'You're such a mum.' His sigh was over-dramatic. 'Always bossing, organising.'

She picked up her chopstick and aimed it like a mini-javelin at his head.

'Joking.'

'Sure.' She got up from the table.

'Where are you going?'

'To get my diary, to work out your next few visits.'

'You're even more of a type A personality than I remember. Joking, really,' he added when he saw the look on her face. 'But I don't have my roster with me.' She raised an eyebrow and tilted her head on one side in disbelief. 'It's true. They're usually done three-monthly. We'll be getting the next one soon, and I'll email it to you with all the times off that I can get here and you can pick what suits. Promise.'

What else could she do? 'How often are you thinking?'

'We work eight weeks on, four off. So I'd like to say I'll come back in each of those blocks of time off but, realistically, probably twice a year for a longish stay?'

She sat down again. 'We'll work it out, Rick. If you're finally on board with this, we'll work it out.'

'Hey, there, monkey.'

Steffi twisted in her chair in time to see Jess hiding behind the door.

'Jess.'

Her little face peeped out. 'I couldn't sleep.'

'How long have you been standing there?'

'I wasn't listening.' But she was grinning from ear to ear. Clearly, she thought she knew something.

'Back to bed.' Jess opened her mouth, ready with another excuse, Steffi knew. 'Now.'

'See you in the morning, Dad?'

'*No,*' said Steffi. 'It's school in the morning.'

'Dad can sleep here so I can see him in the morning.'

'No, Jess, and anyway my stuff's all back at the hotel. I'll work it out with your mum about seeing you after school.'

Her bottom lip dropped but she scooped it back up again when she saw her mother's face, and Steffi knew she was wearing her don't-push-me-any-further look.

She waited until the door closed behind Jess then turned back to their semi-cold dinner, scooping up a prawn. 'So, tell me how a reformed no-hoper gets his kicks on an oil-rig in Saudi?'

'Matt, that doesn't go there, it's got blue on that side.'

It was Jess's third visit in a week and, along with his niece's visits, it was the only bright moment in his life right now. They didn't probe, didn't try to push him to get better, just accepted that his legs weren't working and went on from there.

'So it does.' He hadn't even been looking at the puzzle pieces, and he'd only been half watching Jess do it, too. He'd been wondering since her first visit how to fish for information about her mum and dad—how did you do that without feeling underhanded and mean?

You didn't, he decided, you just had to live with the guilt. 'Is your dad still here?'

Jess slipped another puzzle piece into place and looked up at him for confirmation that she was doing well. He nodded his approval and then she answered. 'Yep. I think he and Mum are going to get married. I heard them talking about working it out. Victoria at school says that's what parents do when they're getting back together.'

What could he say to that?

Jess continued talking, not giving him a chance to respond. 'I've always wanted a dad around. Dads let you do stuff that mums don't.'

'Your mum will still be there, Jess.'

'She won't care. Victoria said Mum will be too busy trying to stay pretty for Dad, she won't mind what I do.'

It seemed he'd been right all along. Steffi did still have feelings for Rick and, no doubt, he himself had helped clarify the situation for her, his accident removing him as a contender. Even if Jess didn't have the full story, they were clearly moving in that direction. Steffi wouldn't let Jess get her hopes up if something wasn't on the cards.

'Mum said to see if you wanted a visitor when she picks me up. Do you?'

He didn't. 'I think you might have worn me out with jigsaws, Jess.'

'That's OK. Your mum said I could go and cook with her if you got tired.' She jumped off the bed. 'I'll do that now, and then you'll be ready for Mum to visit.'

He should never have agreed to Jess visiting him. Maybe he could pretend to be asleep again when Steffi came, but sooner or later his mum would catch him out on that.

As it turned out, he *was* asleep, and as Steffi sat and watched the gentle rise and fall of his chest, she knew that this time, at least, his mother's excuse had been genuine. Which was probably why she'd allowed Steffi into his room in the first place, to slip through the net while Port Cadney's most intractable patient was unaware. Was that what things had come to between them?

She was still sitting on the chair next to his bed when he woke. He opened his eyes to look straight into hers and it seemed like the shutters came down almost in the same instant.

'Did I wake you?'

'No.'

'How are you feeling?'

'I've been better.'

'You've treated me better, too, Matt.'

That startled him, caught him off guard. She knew it probably suited him to avoid dealing with anything more than he had to. But maybe it wasn't doing him any good.

He raked a hand though his hair and she saw that it

was clean—evidence of his mother's home-nursing—but he was pale and thinner even than usual. His grey T-shirt hung from his shoulders, which looked even broader now he'd lost some body weight, and while the colour did nothing for the pallor of his skin, it did amazing things to his clear grey eyes.

She'd thought she may have imagined her strong feelings for him, but the moment she'd looked into his eyes, she'd known beyond a doubt that this was the man she loved.

But the fact that it wasn't mutual was pretty evident in the way he'd already turned his face away from her, concentrating on rearranging the blanket over his legs. This wasn't the Matt she knew.

He glanced at her and turned away again. 'You say I haven't been treating you well.'

She started to rephrase her earlier words. They sounded callous now that they were coming back at her from a man who was dealing with paralysis, but he pressed on and the harshness in his voice rocked her.

'I've had other things going on, Steffi. I'm sorry I haven't spoken to you. But from the sound of things, you've been pretty preoccupied yourself.'

What was he on about now?

'Preoccupied ringing and dropping into see you?' There was anger in her voice now, too, and she gripped the arms of the chair she was sitting in. 'Preoccupied flying down to Adelaide on the first flight I could get, dropping everything to come to you?'

'Let's just leave things, can we, Steffi? You've seen me now, you can see there's nothing more you can do for me. Just leave it at that.'

She gave a short whistle. 'Lying there feeling sorry for yourself is the last thing I thought you'd do, Matt.'

'Is that what you call it? I call it lying here because my bloody legs…' he ripped the blanket off to the side, patches of colour rising in his cheeks, forcing her to look at his legs, long and thin, a little muscle wastage evident already '…don't work.'

Steffi leaned forward in her seat. 'At least you might find anger a more motivating emotion than self-pity.'

'There's a lot more going on than you know.'

'Then why don't you enlighten me instead of shutting me out?' She paused for a moment to soften the tone of her voice and made a conscious effort to loosen her grip on the arms of the chair, to relax her muscles. Getting as hot under the collar as he was wouldn't get them far. 'And if you won't let me help, would you think about seeing a counsellor?'

'You think I need to see a psychologist?' There was derision in his voice.

'I can recommend a good one.' She chewed the inside of her lip, unsure whether to make her admission to Matt or not. She'd made the decision not to previously but maybe, just maybe, it would lend some weight to her suggestion. 'I haven't told you this before but I've been seeing a psychologist myself. I've had some trouble with panic attacks over the last few months.'

He was clearly going to ignore that and she shrugged off the thought that he really didn't seem to care one way or another about her. This was about him, not her. 'So maybe you would benefit, maybe you wouldn't. What's to lose?'

He snorted.

'If you won't consider that, let *me* help you. I'm ready to go through this with you, Matt, every last bit of it.'

'You didn't turn to *me* with your panic attacks, didn't trust *me* enough, Steffi, so don't turn the tables now.'

She tried to interrupt, to explain that that had been different, that they'd only just started seeing each other then and he'd given her the clear message that to admit problems was in itself showing weakness. She'd taken a big risk to confide in him now, but it hadn't paid off. He was rummaging in the drawer next to his bed, ignoring her, and when she tried again, he pulled something out of his drawer and cut her off.

'You can't help. Here.' He thrust a piece of paper at her. 'This is the icing on the cake. In case I don't have enough to deal with.'

His tone was abrasive and Steffi could feel the anger surging out of him, filling the room like a vapour.

She took the paper and quickly scanned it. The letterhead was from a large insurance company, questioning Matt's actions and demanding explanations. Phrases like 'failure to comply with Occupational Health and Safety Standards', 'endangering life', 'resulting in potential for prosecution' and asking for explanations jumped off the page at her.

'I'm sure this is just routine,' she said, hoping she sounded convincing because the letter scared her and had obviously shaken Matt up, too. 'They're just asking for some clarification. Old Jimmy was dead when you reached him, you didn't cause any further harm.'

'Exactly. They'll use that as a reason why I should have waited. They'll say there was nothing I could have done so I shouldn't have put myself at risk. But how could I have waited? I'm bound by my duty of care as a doctor and by the Hippocratic oath to save lives. I had to try.'

'If you put it to them like that, I'm sure they'll have to agree.'

'Don't patronise me.'

'I'm not. I'm trying to be supportive. I thought you

might need your friends around you at the moment. That's what this is all about, Matt. People who care for you just wanting to let you know, wanting to help you.'

'I don't need your pity.'

She stood up, putting the letter on his bedside table. She was never going to get through to him while he was in this mood. 'And I don't need your attitude. So I guess we'll call it even, shall we? Since that's what you so clearly want.' Were those words coming from her mouth?

They were, because he was nodding his agreement, resignation falling back over his face almost visibly to replace the anger that had flared so quickly and harshly just minutes ago.

Her own anger died down as quickly in response, and the sadness that settled in its place seemed to take her one more step away from him. At least when they'd been angry they'd been connected in a way. Now there was only an enormous gulf again.

He closed his eyes and turned his face from her.

So she picked up her bag, packed her heart in ice to start mending later, and left.

She didn't know what else to do.

CHAPTER TEN

'I THINK you're right Steffi,' Jack said. 'It'd be too early for a clinical diagnosis but Matt certainly seems to be in danger of heading for depression.'

Her heart fell. She hadn't wanted to be right about this. Matt's attitude had hurt her but his words were so out of keeping with what she knew about him that she'd felt sure there had to be another influencing factor. Yes, he had a lot to deal with but he didn't have to do it alone. Yet he seemed to want to. She'd voiced her concerns to Jack, making him promise not to mention her name if he spoke to Matt, and now he was agreeing with her diagnosis. She didn't know what was worse—that Matt might be depressed, which now seemed to be the case, or for him to simply not want her near him.

Jack hadn't noticed her mind wandering and was still talking. 'It's not surprising, given what he's been through, but it's stopping him from trying to do things. He'll never get out of that bed if he's not prepared to test the water.'

'You're not suggesting his paralysis is all psychological, are you?'

'Not at all. But I think there's an element of that involved. Depression can manifest in unusual ways. Maybe it's self-doubt on his part, but I do think you're right about his state of mind.'

'What can I do?'

'Just be there for him. Let him know you care.'

'I've tried that. He doesn't want me around, that's pretty clear.'

'He just needs to feel that something is going his way. At the moment he feels everything is conspiring against him. Physically, professionally and emotionally his life is in tatters. His body is damaged, he can't do his beloved work, he's under fire for his handling of the incident and he's not certain about you.'

'He knows how I feel.'

'Have you told him?'

'I…' Steffi paused. Had she? She'd talked about friends gathering around, people who cared about him, and she'd included herself in that. But had she made that clear? In reality her feelings went far deeper than friendship. Did he understand that?

'He thinks you and Rick are reconciling.'

'What?'

'He didn't come straight out and say that but he skirted around the issue, fishing.'

'Where on earth did he get that idea?'

Jack shrugged. 'I don't know but I think he just needs to know if it's true or not. I think that's tearing him apart as much as anything. There's not a lot of incentive for him to get out of bed at the moment.'

This was far more awkward than Steffi had anticipated. It hadn't been hard this time to convince Mrs Zeller to let her into his room, but now she was here, it was clear Matt didn't intend to mention Rick—didn't intend to talk at all—so somehow she had to introduce Rick as a topic of conversation.

I hear you've been asking questions about Rick and me? No. Too abrupt.

Rick's taking Jess fishing this weekend. No. Too insensitive.

Did I tell you that Rick is heading off in a couple of weeks? That might work.

She broke the silence.

'It looks like Rick is going back to Saudi Arabia.'

'By himself?' He looked at her for the first time since she'd come into his room.

'As far as I know.'

'I thought…'

'What?'

'I thought you two were getting back together.'

Jack had been right. 'Why would you think that?'

'Jess said you were working things out.'

'Jess? Working things out?' The penny dropped. 'Working out Rick's trips back to Australia to see Jess. Not working out things between *us*. Believe me, I've got enough on my hands looking after Jess. I don't need to add Rick to my list, too.'

'I must have misunderstood.'

'I think Jess did, too. I'll have to make sure she knows what's going on. She was eavesdropping and obviously she got hold of the wrong end of the stick.'

'It might be a good idea to set things straight.'

He was still sounding stubbornly unmoved and she couldn't help the frustration that flashed through her. She'd sort this out with Jess soon enough, but hadn't she just cleared up the big barrier that had sprung up between *them*? Yet he had nothing to say.

Come on, say something.

She waited. Nothing.

Maybe he hadn't been worried at all. Maybe Jack had misunderstood the focus of Matt's thoughts.

Steffi hid her disappointment.

After all, what had she expected? A declaration of Matt's undying love? For all their problems to be solved after one conversation? For Matt to leap out of bed and claim her for his own? No, none of that. He still had to heal. Physically and emotionally. But she had hoped once he knew there was nothing between Rick and her, he'd at least be happy to see her. Had foolishly hoped, it seemed.

What had she expected?

Matt felt some of the load being lifted from his shoulders with Steffi's news, but there were still so many other problems weighing him down. Was he strong enough to fight them all? He still couldn't walk. What could he possibly offer her and Jess now? Even with Rick apparently out of the running, Steffi still deserved more than he, Matt, could give her. For all sorts of reasons, it just wouldn't work.

Steffi and Jess dumped their bags on the chair in the tiny hallway and headed to the kitchen for a drink. They'd just taken Rick to the airport and although Steffi had braced herself for hysterics from Jess, she'd been calm. Perhaps the knowledge that her father would be back in three months' time was all she'd needed.

Whatever the reason, Steffi was grateful that she didn't have to deal with another drama. Matt had continued to shut her out even after their discussion and Steffi was at her wits' end. Maybe she'd have to accept their relationship was over, but how could she then continue to live in the town where there were so many memories of her time with Matt?

She hadn't found time to get back to Adelaide to sort out their house yet. Was that a sign? The support finally coming in from Rick would now make living in Adelaide possible, but she couldn't move Jess again, not when she was settled and happy here. Besides, they were content in their little unit and Steffi was enjoying her job. All in all, they were better off in Port Cadney. Even with her bruised and battered heart.

As Jess drained the last of her juice, Steffi turned her thoughts to more immediate concerns.

'What do you say to fish and chips tonight?'

'Can I have a hamburger instead?'

'Sure. Let me get changed out of my uniform and we'll go and get dinner.'

'Could we take it down to the beach?'

The beach. A vision of Matt playing in the surf with Jess and Susie sprang to mind. Would it always be like this? Unexpected images of Matt appearing with any mention of times shared? She couldn't avoid *all* these places.

'I guess we can go to Main Beach.' Anywhere but The Cove where they'd gone with Matt and Susie.

'Cool.'

Steffi kissed the top of her daughter's head as she headed for her room to get changed. The telephone rang as she walked past.

'Hello.'

'Stephanie, hello. I've been trying to reach you but I don't like to leave messages on those machines.'

It wasn't hard to place the voice. 'Mrs Zeller. Is everything all right?'

'Yes, dear, everything's fine. I just wondered when you were planning on visiting Mattias again. We haven't seen you for a while.'

Was that a reproach? 'He's made it clear he doesn't want to see me.'

'I know I said to be patient, but I think now he's had enough time. He got some good news in the mail today. I thought it might be a good day to see him.'

'I'm taking Jess out for dinner in a while. Could we

call in after that? I don't want to change our plans at this late stage.' Jess had always been her number-one priority and she wasn't going to drop everything for Matt. Not any more.

'Hello, Jessica. This is a lovely surprise.' Matt's mother greeted them at the door, feigning ignorance of their visit.

So she hasn't told Matt we were coming, then, Steffi registered. What's going on?

'We've come to see Matt. It's been ages, I've got loads to tell him.' Jess raced down the hallway, quite at home. She's probably spent more time here than me, Steffi thought.

'Mattias is out by the pool.' Mrs Zeller called out after Jess. Steffi gave her a questioning look. 'His father organised a wheelchair. Said it was time to stop moping about the place and get out of bed. His father can't stand to see a problem with no solution. In his view, life is always much simpler than we make it, you just have to stop complaining and get on with it.'

That sounded like the attitude his dad had instilled into Matt early on. 'And so he got into the chair? Just like that?'

'No. Mattias wouldn't have it in his room. Kept ordering his father to take it out, but Nic kept refusing. Told him he'd have to do it himself. So it's sat there for the last two days until the physio came. She got Mattias into it. He's still not himself but this is a start, and I think the letter that came today may help things, too.'

They reached the French doors that opened to the garden and Steffi could see Jess examining Matt's wheelchair, asking questions with the innocence of an eight-year-old. He was smiling at Jess, and Steffi thought she'd never seen a more beautiful sight.

'Look, Mum. Isn't this awesome?'

Matt looked up at Jess's exclamation. His smile disappeared, all life and laughter gone from his face in the blink of an eye.

It had been a mistake to come.

'Come on, Jess, darling. I don't think Matt wants visitors right now.'

'Nonsense.' Mrs Zeller's brisk voice cut in. 'Sit down, Stephanie, Jess. Tell Matt what you've been up to while I put the kettle on.'

So they did. At least, Jess did. She chatted away and Matt responded to her, asking about her netball practice and swimming lessons while Steffi sat frozen to the spot, like a garden ornament, trying to blend into the bushes.

'We took Dad to the airport today. He's going back to Arabia,' Jess informed Matt. Steffi was watching him, waiting for his reaction, when his gaze flew up, catching her by surprise. For a brief moment she thought she saw hope in his grey eyes.

'He's gone?'

Steffi nodded. 'I told you he was going.'

'Yes, you did.' And then he smiled at her. Not quite the real McCoy, bona fide Matt smile she knew so well, but the closest he'd sent her way since he'd been in hospital, and it warmed the cold water she'd been encouraging to turn into ice around her heart. For a moment it seemed like it might be possible for everything to be all right. And then the shutters came down again.

'Here we are.' Mrs Zeller returned, bearing a tray with steaming cups of coffee. 'Jessica, dear, how would you like to come for a walk with me to the shop for an ice cream? I seem to have run out.' She pulled an envelope out of her apron pocket, handing it to Matt. 'I thought you might like to show this to Stephanie. Come on, Jessica.'

'What is it?' Steffi asked as the others departed.

'A letter from the insurance company.'

Good news, his mother had said. 'What does it say?'

'It says…' Matt pulled the letter out and unfolded it '…they accept my version of events as being a, quote, "true and accurate record" and they won't be pressing any charges or recommending any further action be taken.'

'That's fantastic news. It must be a load off your mind.' She wanted to leap out of her chair, hug him, but there was still an imaginary sign above his head, saying 'keep away', even if it was written in smaller letters now.

'It's one less thing to worry about.'

Jack had said Matt just needed to feel as if some things were going his way and then he might be able to haul himself out of the doldrums. This had to be a step in the right direction.

'You're a terrific doctor. Don't start questioning your abilities and commitment because of all this.'

'I'm not. I'd do the same thing again if I had to. But…' he gave a wry laugh as he looked at his lap '…that's the irony. I probably wouldn't be able to do it again.'

'Oh, Matt.' Steffi felt her heart tearing as she looked at his glum face. 'Why won't you let me help you?'

'It's not that easy.'

'Yes, it is.' She only had one more thing to offer. She had to put her cards on the table. It was now or never, because Jack had been right when he'd suggested she hadn't ever told Matt how she felt. 'I should have told you this before, Matt.' She swallowed hard. This declaration-of-love scenario was quite an ordeal when you had nothing to give you confidence in a happy outcome. 'I love you, Matt, and I need you. All I want is your love in return. Can't you give me that?'

'No.'

His answer was so blunt it took her a moment to process, and before she'd quite worked through the rejection he was talking again.

'Why can't you see it? I have nothing to offer you. Nothing.'

'You're still the same person you were when you went down the mine. I loved you then and I love you still. Nothing's changed that. I just should have told you earlier.'

'I refuse to be a burden to you, a liability. You need a partner, not someone else who depends on you. You said that yourself.'

'I said what?'

'You said, "Jess is enough responsibility, I don't want to add Rick to my list too."'

'And I meant it. I don't want to look after Rick. I don't love him, I love *you*. We can get through these obstacles. Your paralysis is only temporary—you'll walk again.'

'And if I don't?'

'It won't matter.'

'It matters to me.'

'If that's more important than loving me, there's nothing else I can say.' Steffi gathered up their mugs, cold anger turning her face to a mask, and placed them on the tray to carry it back into the house. 'Or do.' She had some pride. OK, so it was covered by a fairly thick layer of stupidity, putting her heart out there like that when anyone could see she was begging for it to be trampled on. But there was still some pride there, some instinct for self-preservation.

Jess and Mrs Zeller were just coming outside, Jess's face liberally covered with chocolate ice cream, as Steffi reached the back door. Matt said nothing. She hadn't made eye contact with him and he'd said nothing, done nothing, to make her stay.

'Hi, sweetie, did you get *any* ice cream into your mouth?' Steffi dug through her bag, searching for a tissue to wipe Jess's face, trying to get her emotions under control before it became obvious how upset she was.

'How are things here?' Mrs Zeller asked, and Steffi could feel a pair of assessing eyes on her, so she may as well come clean.

'I can't get through to him. He's not ready to listen to me.' She crouched down to wipe Jess's mouth.

'Maybe he just needs more time.'

She shrugged. 'I'm not sure. He has to *want* to get better and something's stopping him. I thought I knew what it was, but it seems I was wrong. I can't force him to see me, to let me help him.'

Steffi grabbed Jess's hand as she went to say goodbye to Matt. 'Matt's tired, sweetheart, just wave goodbye.' Together they walked inside and headed for the front door.

As they stepped onto the front verandah, the older woman patted her arm. 'I hoped he would be feeling more positive by now, especially with the news today.'

'What's that funny humming noise, Mum?'

Steffi looked up and saw the eaves of the verandah were thick with swarming bees. 'Quick, Jess, back inside.' As she turned to usher her daughter into the house, bees flew about her face and she swatted at them and simultaneously felt a sting on her index finger and cheek. She just managed to get inside and slam the door.

'I've been stung, get Matt, hurry, allergic.' Steffi struggled to speak the last few words. Her lips were already swelling and her throat thickening as the histamines spread through her.

She heard Mrs Zeller direct Jess to fetch Matt and say

she'd call the ambulance, but that was all background noise to the fear that was pounding in her brain. She'd had rapid swelling when she'd only been stung on the foot, so stings to the face put her in real danger. Her heart racing, she slid down the hallway wall until her lower back was leaning against the skirting-board and focused her concentration on breathing.

It must have only been a minute or two before Matt reached her, but by then her eyes had been forced shut by the swelling. She could hear him but could see nothing.

'It's all right, Steffi, I'm here now. I've got adrenalin in my bag, I'll give you an injection.'

She heard him rummage in his bag, talking all the while. 'Jess is out the back with Mum. OK, here's the needle. That's it. Mum's called the ambulance but you'll feel better before they get here.' Steffi could already feel her heart rate slowing but her swollen lips were still making speech impossible. 'I'm taking your blood pressure and pulse now.'

It was amazing how the fear started to recede as soon as she felt Matt's fingers on her arm. Her thoughts were fuzzy but she was conscious of a sadness that she hadn't been able to give that feeling of safety, trust, back to him.

'Pulse 110. BP 100 over 60. A bit low—is that normal for you?'

Steffi shook her head. It was normally 120 over 70 but she couldn't tell him that.

'I'll keep checking it. You tell me when it hits normal.' Matt continued to record her blood pressure as it continued to rise slowly so that by the time the ambulance arrived it was close to normal.

'Connor's here now.' Steffi heard Matt talking with the paramedic, although they seemed a long way away.

'She's had an anaphylactic reaction, now under control.

I've administered adrenalin and her heart rate and BP are approaching normal.'

'Put her on oxygen?'

'Yes, and admit her overnight for observation.'

'Righto. Let's get moving. We'll pop you on the stretcher, Steffi. Just relax.'

Then Matt's voice again, closer now, just as Steffi felt herself being slid across onto the cool sheets of the stretcher. 'Mum and I'll bring Jess with us and we'll call your parents on the way.'

'You gave us all quite a scare.' Matt wheeled himself into her hospital room just after breakfast next morning. 'How are you feeling?'

She raised a hand to her face, looking self-conscious. The swelling had receded, although there were still some red blotches on her skin.

'You look beautiful.'

Gingerly, she touched her cheek. 'I doubt it, but thank you anyway.' Matt was the last person she'd expected to see here. And the first one she'd have wanted to visit her.

He manoeuvred himself over to her bed. 'We could so easily have lost you. You need to carry an epi-pen or an inhaler. You can't risk something like that happening again.'

'I've got an inhaler in my handbag but I wasn't thinking clearly, it all happened so fast. You saved my life. Thank you seems so inadequate but—thank you.'

He took in her face, set off by her high brow and azure eyes. Brushed his gaze over her lips, the top one almost as wide and full as the bottom—her features overall perhaps too strong in such a small face but somehow they worked, and, to him, she was beautiful. 'I'll never let anything happen to you.'

'That's quite a promise when you won't let me near you.'

He could see the wariness in her eyes and hear it in her voice, and he didn't blame her. 'I know I was stubborn.'

'It's not too late to remedy that. I'm here to stay if you want me.' Her voice was still cagey, as if she was only game to dip one toe into the uncharted waters of their relationship, a relationship he'd been doing his best to tear apart until now.

He took her hand in his. 'I thought I had nothing to offer you.'

'I've told you, all I want is your love.'

He grinned at her but he didn't answer, didn't want to just yet. Instead, he stood and took a single step to her side and sat on the edge of her bed. She sat straight up, her mouth falling open, and he saw the amazement in her eyes at what he'd just done.

'Matt, you can stand!'

His grin widened. 'And walk. After a fashion.'

'Why didn't you tell me?'

'I didn't know until yesterday.'

'Don't keep me in suspense, Matt, *tell* me.'

'When you were stung, there wasn't time to waste. I had to get to my bag for the adrenalin.' He waved a hand in the direction of his wheelchair. 'That's too cumbersome. It got me down the hallway but when I saw you on the floor, it was an automatic response to get out of it. Not that I knew I was doing it. Jess noticed. I suppose it was a reflex action, a subconscious thought, much like me thinking I couldn't walk.'

'Why didn't you walk in here today?'

'My legs are still weak, too much lying around, and I can't walk too far yet. And then there was the surprise element. I couldn't let that slip past.'

'I'll give you that. You nailed the surprise element.' She sank back against the pillows. He could see she was tired and while there was delight in her face, she was still holding herself a little aloof from him, not at all surprising when the offer of her love was still hanging unacknowledged between them.

'Up for another surprise?'

'That's not enough for one day?'

'I'm hoping you'll like this one just as much.'

He was grinning as he pulled a white packet from his pocket and held it out to her. 'Open it.'

She did.

'Oh.' Her disappointment was plain to see but she was doing her best to mask it. 'An epi-pen.'

'Much better than an inhaler when your allergy is so severe, and I gathered yesterday you didn't have one.'

She nodded.

'And there's something else.'

Was that a flash of hope in her eyes?

'Bear with me, it might take a while.'

'Go on.'

He reached out across the sheets and took her hand in his, stroking the backs of her fingers with his. 'I've been a stubborn, grumpy fool, thinking I can get through everything on my own, not wanting to be a burden to you. I thought I was protecting you by not letting you near, but when I came so close to losing you I realised how you must have felt when I had my accident.'

He took a breath, marshalling his thoughts. He was usually measured with his words but now he had quite a speech to get through and he needed to get it right. 'I didn't understand how you could love me, I didn't see why you would. I've never felt like I've really belonged anywhere, but when I'm with you I feel like I've come home. And if you feel remotely like I do then we have enough love between us to get through anything.'

He leant in towards her, pressing her hand against his chest and covering it with his own. 'I know I've taken my time and messed things up pretty badly, but I'm hoping I'm not too late to tell you that I love you and nothing would make me happier than to marry you.'

'Are you sure?'

'What kind of answer is that? I promise we'll have a beautiful life together, the three of us. Maybe we'll even have a tribe of siblings for Jess. What do you say?'

Her eyes were shining. 'When can I get out of here?'

'One more thing then we'll go home.'

He pulled another small bag from his pocket and tipped it up, emptying something into his hand. Uncurling his fingers, flashes of fiery colour sparkled from his palm. He picked up a smooth oval stone between his thumb and forefinger, holding it up to the light. Brilliant colour spilled out, rich emerald, sapphire and ruby, all intermingled.

'This opal was cut from the first one I ever found. I've never found a better one. I'd like to have it made into an engagement ring for you.' He handed her the stone and she cradled it in her palm, looking from the gem back to him and back to the gem again.

'That's the loveliest gift anyone has ever thought to give me. It even tops the epi-pen.' He joined her laughter. 'I'd be honoured to wear it.'

Again he tipped the packet and this time a much smaller but no less brilliant stone slid out. 'This comes from the same rock. I thought we'd have it set in a pendant for Jess, so she knows what an important part of this she is.'

'That's a beautiful idea, she'll be thrilled. Thank you.' Her smile told him everything his gesture meant to her.

'You know, you're going to make a wonderful father to the hordes of children we'll have together.'

'About that…'

'Yes?'

'I can't say I'm in a hurry to get back down those mines to find another opal, so how about we have a boy first?'

'You think he'll be happy with a toy car or something easy like that?'

'A man can hope.'

'And so…' she threw back the sheets and shifted next to him so he could envelop her in his arms '…it seems, can a woman.'

Matt dropped a kiss on the top of her head. 'Happy?'

'Blissful.'

'In that case, get ready to be happy for the rest of your life.' He stood momentarily and pressed the nurse's call-bell behind the bed. 'Let's get you out of here. Eternity won't be long enough to show you what you mean to me, so we need to get home and make a start right now.'

'Home. Right now. Wonderful words.'

'I know some that are even better.' He tucked her hair behind her ear and brought his mouth close to whisper, 'I love you with all my heart, Steffi Harrison-soon-to-be-Zeller.'

Steffi placed her hand against the line of his jaw and turned his mouth to hers for a kiss that left her in no doubt of his love.

And when the nurse on duty responded to the call-bell, neither noticed as she came into the room. And neither noticed when she left just as quietly. Their life together had started and they both knew it would be everything they'd ever hoped for. And more.

MILLS & BOON®

Live the emotion

0105/03b

Medical
romance™

THE BABY DOCTOR'S DESIRE *by Kate Hardy*

(London City General)

When two caring doctors cannot deny – but cannot let on! – that they're attracted to each other, their only option is to have a secret affair. But for maternity consultant Kieran Bailey keeping his relationship with Dr Judith Powell private proves impossible. And if their secret is exposed the consequences will be huge…!

THE DOCTORS' BABY BOND *by Abigail Gordon*

When her stepsister's newborn son is orphaned Dr Andrina Bell doesn't hesitate to step in as his mum. Drew Curtis, country GP and the baby's uncle, wants the best for his nephew too. When he offers Andrina a job and a home she knows she can't refuse. But falling for Drew's charm and kindness in every way – was never part of the arrangement…

THE FLIGHT DOCTOR'S RESCUE *by Laura Iding*

(Air Rescue)

When her ex-fiancé's family offered to buy her unborn baby, Shelly's response was to run! Now, under a different name, flight nurse Shelly is making a new life for herself and her child. But there's something about one of her new colleagues… Flight doctor Jared O'Connor not only makes Shelly's pulse race, he has the same surname as her son's father!

On sale 4th February 2005

Available at most branches of WHSmith, Tesco, ASDA, Martins, Borders, Eason, Sainsbury's and all good paperback bookshops.

Visit www.millsandboon.co.uk

4 FREE

BOOKS AND A SURPRISE GIFT!

We would like to take this opportunity to thank you for reading this Mills & Boon® book by offering you the chance to take FOUR more specially selected titles from the Medical Romance™ series absolutely FREE! We're also making this offer to introduce you to the benefits of the Reader Service™—

- ★ FREE home delivery
- ★ FREE gifts and competitions
- ★ FREE monthly Newsletter
- ★ Exclusive Reader Service offers
- ★ Books available before they're in the shops

Accepting these FREE books and gift places you under no obligation to buy, you may cancel at any time, even after receiving your free shipment. Simply complete your details below and return the entire page to the address below. You don't even need a stamp!

YES! Please send me 4 free Medical Romance books and a surprise gift. I understand that unless you hear from me, I will receive 6 superb new titles every month for just £2.69 each, postage and packing free. I am under no obligation to purchase any books and may cancel my subscription at any time. The free books and gift will be mine to keep in any case.

M5ZED

Ms/Mrs/Miss/Mr ....Initials ....
                                                                    BLOCK CAPITALS PLEASE
Surname ....

Address ....

....

....Postcode..................................

Send this whole page to:
UK: FREEPOST CN81, Croydon, CR9 3WZ